The Herring Girls

I took the sharpest knife from my pocket and picked up a good-sized fish, trying hard to remember what Hannah had taught me. I pushed the knife in carefully and twisted it, and the guts flew out into the gut tub.

The man grunted. "Now size?" he snapped.

"Mattiefull," I answered him, my voice all shaky.

"What?" He put his hand to his ear.

"Mattiefull," I said it loudly.

He nodded and pointed to the basket behind me. I slipped the fish in and snatched up another herring to gut.

Nelly pushed in beside me and set to work. Mary Jane went to pack the barrel behind us.

I paused to watch Nelly for a moment and my mouth dropped open. Nelly could certainly gip, and she could gip fast. She'd done four fish while I did one.

"Stop gawping," she muttered under her breath. "Get gipping!"

Theresa Tomlinson

The Herring Girls

RED FOX

A Red Fox Book

Published by Random House Children's Books
20 Vauxhall Bridge Road, London SW1V 2SA

A division of Random House UK Ltd
London Melbourne Sydney Auckland
Johannesburg and agencies throughout the world

1 3 5 7 9 10 8 6 4 2

First published by Julia MacRae 1994

Red Fox edition 1996

Printed and bound in Great Britain by
Cox & Wyman Ltd, Reading, Berkshire

RANDOM HOUSE UK Limited Reg. No. 954009

Papers used by Random House UK Limited
are natural, recyclable products made from wood grown in
sustainable forests. The manufacturing processes conform to
the environmental regulations of the country of origin.

ISBN 0 09 936311 9

Dedicated to all the herring girls, coopers, fishermen, and landladies who worked with the North Sea herring fleet.

Theresa Tomlinson books published by Red Fox

The Forestwife
The Herring Girls

Author's Note

The character of the picture man is based on the Whitby photographer Frank Meadow Sutcliffe, whilst the old lifeboatman is based on Henry Freeman, sole survivor of the 1861 Whitby lifeboat disaster, though as far as I know his boat the *Louie Becket* was never trapped behind the East Pier as described in the story. Mrs Dryden Smith – Trickey – was a real fisherwoman who lived in Henrietta Street, and was well known for her crafty ways; she appeared in the film, *The Turn of the Tide*. Thomas Langlands was the Whitby lifeboat coxswain in 1902, and for many years after.

Mr Bill Fortune is the fourth generation of a family of fish smokers, still smoking herrings in Henrietta Street. All the other characters in the story are fictitious, though very much inspired by Frank Meadow Sutcliffe's photographs. I hope that Scottish readers will forgive me for the use of 'Scotch' throughout the story. 'Scotch' was the word that would have been used in Whitby at the turn of the century, and the herring pickling process was known as 'the Scotch cure'.

"Bread on the waters! Like manna it was!
One hour nothing, the next enough to feed a town, and
the sky all lit up with the reflection of the shoal."

Joe Tomlinson – North Sea fisherman

Chapter 1

It was late in July; one of those days of sun and heavy showers, worse for us than steady rain. Our mam's the washerwoman and when there's sun we carry the washing up to the lines on Top Green, and when it rains we have to fetch it down again.

I went with Robbie and Alice and we pegged the first lot of clothes and linen out to dry, but even before we got back to our yard, the sky darkened and great spots of rain came pelting down on us. I shook my fist up at the grey clouds and got my eyes sploshed full of rain.

"Away back and fetch the clothes in," I said.

We set about the washing, all wet and angry, throwing the clean sheets and petticoats wildly into our baskets.

"Ger'outa my way," I yelled, as Alice reached for the same white sheet as me.

"Great Gawk!" she screamed. "Lanky Dory! You've stuck your elbow in my eye. See what she's done to me, Robbie!"

"Shut up! Daft lasses!" Robbie cried. "You've forgotten Mrs Metcalfe's fine pillow case, our Dory."

I leapt at the pillowcase, careless of the peg that held it, and as I snatched it down the fine lace edging ripped.

We went quiet then, standing there in the soaking rain.

"Mam'll play war with us," I whispered.

I think we knew then that it would be a bad day.

Mam was bending over the dolly tub, her face and hands bright red through the steam. She groaned when she saw us back, the damp clothes heaped up in our baskets.

"It's all Lanky Dory's fault," Alice cried. "She never turned

1

her boots to Whitby Abbey last night, though I kept on telling her to. She's brought this rain and she's ripped Mrs Metcalfe's best pillowcase."

Mam pushed the wet hair away from her forehead with the back of her hand.

"Stop it," she snapped. "Stop teasing our Dorothy so. This rain is none of her fault and if she's ripped a pillowcase, then she shall mend it. We'll just have to grit our teeth and do the best we can. Rob, take the bairns and sit on the step with them. You big girls hang up the linen. We shall have to use the loft, I dare say."

I whispered low to Alice as we climbed up the ladder. "Miss Hindmarch says it's ignorant to think that turning your boots to the abbey'll bring us fine weather. Ignorant, she says."

We spent the whole morning setting up drying lines all over our small cottage and getting crosser than ever. We ended up with a whole day's washing still wet, and in danger of getting itself dirty again. Then at last after midday, the sun came out properly, and we were able to carry some of the washing back up to Top Green.

By late afternoon Mam was still wringing out clothes. Old Mrs Wright had kindly stopped by for a while to turn the handle of the mangle for us, and Alice was lifting petticoats, fresh from the starch tub. The smell of fresh baked bread and fried taties drifted from our neighbours' doorways, but we went hungry.

"Lanky Dory should be doing this," Alice grumbled. "She's biggest and strongest, and my stomach's empty."

I stuck my tongue out at her. She knows how I hate to be called Lanky Dory, just because I'm tall.

"Stop it!" Mam bellowed. She was red in the face, she was that vexed. "Stop that noise, Alice, you'll feel the flat of my hand." Then she turned to me, and managed to bring a kinder sound to her voice. "Will you run up to the lines

again, honey, and check if there's owt that's dry? I'll make us a bit of tea for when you get back."

My shoulders drooped at the thought of the hill again, and Alice gave a nasty low laugh as I went to the door.

Though the paving stones and grass were soaking wet, strong sunlight warmed our twisting narrow streets and mist rose everywhere.

I checked the lines, and I found three sheets that were ready for ironing, but then I couldn't face going straight back to our Alice's piping voice and the dank fog of steam that filled our kitchen. I sat down on the edge of the green looking out towards the sea.

I only meant to stay there for a moment or two, but the warm summery wind was fresh on my face. It was peaceful up there, and I could look down onto the busy staithe, and watch the cobles coming back with the tide.

Seagulls swooped down towards the boats, mewing like cats, while the fishermen jumped out into the shallows and splashed thigh deep through the waves, to haul their cobles up onto the shingle.

Our Rob was down there on the staithe with the little ones. I knew what they were after – they'd be begging for fresh boiled crab claws.

A gang of women were gathering on the top staithe, and setting up tin baths and buckets over fires well stacked with driftwood. A cloud of steam rose above them, while the women shouted at the bairns to keep back.

Dan Welford had a good catch of crabs, I could see by the careful way that he lifted the waving claws from the wooden crib of his boat.

I made myself turn away and started to gather in the dry washing, folding it carefully to try to please my mam. I sniffed at it and smiled; it smelt of the sea. Then as I turned to go I glanced back down to the top staithe, and I had to stare again.

Mr Welford and his wife were leaning on the wooden rail
and they'd got their six-month-old grandson, Joby, in a fishing basket between them. He peeped over the top like a
laughing, wriggling fish. They smiled, but they held themselves quite still. A few yards back from them, a tall man
with a beard bent over a wooden box that stood on three
thin legs. I knew him at once; we all knew him. He was the
Whitby photographer, who tramped about the villages with
his camera and his black capes and his folding camera legs.
We called him the picture man.

I could see what a fine sight they made, though thick
white mist rose from the sea behind them and blotted out
the view of the cottages on the far side of the beck.

The picture man waved his arm and pointed, and our
Rob went sliding along the rail to sit by Mrs Welford. Their
Billy and our young Nan crept up on the other side. I knew
that Rob'd be pleased as punch to be put into that picture.
They held themselves still as can be for a moment or two,
gathered around the laughing baby.

5

Then all at once the picture was made, and Mr and Mrs Welford were bending down to their baskets to sort out the crabs and lobsters. Our Robbie went to help them as I knew he would. He'd hang around the Welfords for hours, would Rob; anything to do with fishing and you could bet he'd be there in the thick of it.

I started back to our cottage, suddenly sad. I understood our Robbie well enough, for I wished that I was one of the Welfords too; and part of a big busy fishing family.

I wanted it to be my dad, guiding his coble through the sea roads towards Sandwick staithe. I wanted it to be my dad, waving and calling out my name in his deep rumbling voice.

Our mam, Annie Lythe, hasn't always been a washer-woman, and as I'm the eldest I can remember the times when my dad came back from the sea with his lines dripping with cod and ling and haddock.

It was hard work then, for each day we'd have to fix up my dad's lines and fetch the bait, but we used to gossip and laugh with the other families while we worked. Then that terrible spring day came, when the tides were high and the sea was wild and changeable.

Dan Welford had come back at midday, rowing hard against the tide, and the rest of the cobles following, so that all the village ran down to the staithe knowing there must be trouble. They'd seen my dad and his brother Bob with their sail flapping loose and heading dangerously close to Hobs Head rocks. They'd gone to their aid as fast as they could, but our coble smashed into the rocks and, by the time the Welfords had reached them, there was nowt to be found but splinters of broken mast by the wrecked coble and their flat fishing baskets floating on the water.

Dan Welford has always said that it takes three men to handle a coble and see to the lines. But my dad and his young brother were independent that way. Stubborn was what Mam called it.

Since that day, our mam has kept all six of us from the workhouse by rubbing and scouring at other folks' clothes. The vicar up at Hinderwell raised a bit of money and presented her with a strong iron mangle. So our cottage is filled with steam and the strong smell of Naptha soap that makes our eyes water. But we don't want the workhouse, nothing could be as bad as that.

We try not to grumble, but we don't like it much. I used to carry fish baskets down to the staithe, not washing to the lines. I'd give anything to go running to help my dad with his catch, and beg a ride up the hill on his shoulders as I used to, twisting my fingers into the stiff salty hairs of his beard.

I sighed as I reached our doorstep. My dad would not know me now for I'd grown too tall to ride on anyone's shoulders.

Though Mam had managed to make us some tea and bread and dripping, she was still very fussed and couldn't listen to the excited chatter of Rob and the bairns, who burst in with tales of being photographed. One of the lines in our yard had snapped, and freshly washed shirts and bloomers had gone down into the mud and must be washed again.

I sighed at the thought of it, but I knew she must be done in.

"Shall I scrub them for you, Mam?"

"Nay, lass," she said, giving my hand a squeeze. "I fear you must traipse up to Top Green again, for we've still got Mrs Metcalfe's linen up there, and Alice – you shall have to fetch more water from the spring."

When I got up to Top Green I found the picture man there, crouching beside our washing lines, struggling to get his camera fixed up so that it pointed out to sea across the bay.

He stopped and doffed his hat as soon as I reached the lines. He was like that; treated a fishwife or even a washerwoman as if she were a lady, though he'd a bit of a chuckle in his voice.

"Am I in your way?" he asked.

I shook my head, gone all shy.

"I've been watching for that sight all week," he said, his voice deep with pleasure and excitement. "There they go . . . chasing the silver darlings."

I was puzzled for a moment, but then as I looked out to sea, I understood.

Dark sails appeared on the horizon, heading out to sea from Whitby harbour. Just two or three at first, then quickly the skyline was filled with them. It was the herring fleet, sailing off to the fishing grounds where the herring shoals swim up to the surface at this time of year.

Chapter 2

I smiled, for we look forward each summer to the coming of the herring fleet. The Whitby fishermen are joined by the Scotch boats, and by others from all along the coast. They even come from Cornwall. Whitby is suddenly bursting with strangers and noise and bustle.

"Won't all that thick white mist spoil your picture?" I asked, forgetting my shyness.

The picture man smiled and shook his head.

"There's many a fine photographer would agree with you, but not me; I love that mist." Then he sighed. "The boats are moving too fast, they've a good wind behind them. I should have brought my new box camera that can snap a picture quick as a flash. There's more than twenty boats out there, and I've heard there's others expected. It looks as though there'll be herrings in Whitby tomorrow."

"Aye," I told him. "I went last summer, and I saw it all. I saw the coopers and the dealers and the herring girls. Miss Hindmarch took me."

"Did she now?" He smiled at me with interest. "And what did you think of it?"

"A fine old carry on," I told him.

He laughed. "You're right about that."

Miss Hindmarch is the kindest teacher in our school, and I think she was quite shocked when she found out that I'd never been to Whitby.

"What, Dory? A big girl like you and never been to Whitby?"

"Mam cannot spare me," I whispered, suddenly shamed. The truth was I'd never been further than Hinderwell.

Miss Hindmarch called in at our cottage, and she fixed it up with Mam. She took me into Whitby on the next Saturday. It was the best day of my life.

We walked down Flowergate, and I went wild with excitement at the smells and the hubbub of the busy shops. But then I looked out across the harbour to the great abbey high above us on the clifftops and I suddenly stopped. I could do nothing but stare up at those still grey stones, set all about in green, high above the jumbled houses.

Miss Hindmarch asked me what was wrong. I couldn't think what to say to her for I've never been one for clever talk. I blinked and shook my head, then I whispered, "I think that must be heaven up there."

Miss Hindmarch laughed and hugged me. "Have you ever had ice-cream?" she asked.

It was when we walked down towards the pier looking for the ice-cream stall that we saw the herring girls, and what a sight they were; big strong lasses every one of them, standing behind great troughs piled high with silver herrings. Farlanes those troughs were called, Miss Hindmarch told me so. The girls worked like lightning, gutting the fish and slipping them into baskets behind them. Some worked as packers, snatching up the herrings from the baskets, two fish in each hand. They went so fast you couldn't see the fish clearly, or know how they did it.

They shouted, in loud roaring voices, "One pair, two pair, three pair, four . . ."

"Tally!" another girl bellowed.

Then someone started counting all over again.

The strong-smelling fish guts fouled their oilskin aprons, and spattered their arms. I stared open-mouthed at them, such a wild and frightening lot they were. Miss Hindmarch laughed at my amazement. She shook her head.

"There's no one works like those Scottish girls," she said.

The picture man gave up trying to make a photograph of the fast-moving fleet, and he began packing up his camera and boxes.

"That's enough for today," he said. "The light's fading."

I set to helping him, and I lifted his wooden camera legs over the green, looking about for the pony and trap that I'd expected to find.

"How shall you get home?" I asked.

"Why, I shall tramp along to Hinderwell station as I usually do," he told me. "There's the evening train due in half an hour."

"What? And carry all these boxes and things."

"Oh, I expect I shall manage," he smiled.

"I'll help you carry them down the lane," I insisted. The picture man was well known for handing out pennies, and he did not disappoint me, for when I turned back at the end of our lane, he felt deep into his pockets and pulled out three shining pennies and a farthing. I think he'd given me all that was left in his pockets, for he turned them both out and found his return ticket at the bottom.

"Yes, that's all for today."

I thanked him politely and he bowed to me and touched his hat.

"It is a shame that the light has gone or I might have made a photograph of you," he said, looking down at me thoughtfully. "Yes, that would be good. A young fisher girl sitting on the bank, watching the herring boats in the distance."

"I fear I'm not really a fisher girl," I said, feeling shy again. "I'm the washerwoman's daughter. You wouldn't want a great lanky lass like me in your picture."

"Lanky?" he said loudly. "Who calls you lanky?"

"My sister does," I whispered, wishing that I'd kept quiet. "All the school children do."

"I'd not call you lanky," he spoke soft now. "I'd call you tall and strong like me. I think it grand to be tall. You can see what others cannot."

I smiled at him then, and waved as he walked on towards Hinderwell, his wooden camera legs swinging from a shoulder strap.

I sat there back on Top Green after the picture man had gone, watching the yellow flickering lights of the herring fleet and thinking of all the gutting that should be done in the morning.

Then suddenly I jumped up trembling and started grabbing dry sheets from the lines. The herring drifters in the distance had lit their riding lights. I'd sat up there staring stupidly out to sea while darkness gathered around me. Mam would go mad.

As I leapt down the steps from the green, my arms full of folded linen, I saw our Alice coming stumbling up the steep pathway.

"Oh, she'll love to see me in deep trouble," I muttered. "I'm coming, I'm coming," I yelled, cursing myself for being so dreamy and daft.

But Alice did not look pleased or gloating. Her face was white and frightened. She burst into tears when she saw me.

"Oh, Dory, I've been shouting and shouting for you. I'm that scared and I don't know what to do. Something terrible has happened to our mam."

I stared at her, my heart thundering in my chest, and my arms so full of piled-up linen that I couldn't run without dropping it.

"Here . . . take these off me . . . take 'em quick!"

Alice knuckled the tears from her eyes and held out her arms obediently. Then we both skidded down the steep bank to our cottage as fast as we could.

The stone-flagged floor of our kitchen was awash with soapy water. The big earthenware dolly tub had tipped over and cracked and Mam lay awkwardly beside it on the floor, her hair all soaked in the dirty water. Little Nan crouched in the wet beside her, pulling at her shoulder. Polly stood by the table, staring white-faced at them both.

"Mam's fallen down with a great bang," she sobbed. "She won't get up and she's getting her frock all wet and dirty."

I almost dropped the dry clean clothes I was so scared, but I made myself put them down safely on the table, for nothing vexed Mam more than clean clothes soiled again. Then I ran paddling through the mess to help her.

Mam's eyes rolled and a horrible gurgling sound came from her throat, her mouth slewed over to one side of her face.

"She cannot get up," Alice cried. "I've tried to pull her up, but she cannot."

It was terrible to see my big strong mam, struggling and helpless on the floor like that, and I looked wildly about, wondering where best to get help. Our closest neighbour was Hannah and her husband, Frank, more members of the big Welford family. We call her Aunt Hannah, but then so does half the bay, and Hannah can be very sharp spoken if you're fooling about. But I knew that this was no time to be fearing a telling off, and Hannah would always help when it was really needed.

I ran then and started hammering on her door.

"Hannah, Hannah," I screamed. "Please help us; Mam's took badly."

There was no sound from inside and then I remembered that she'd still be down on the staithe, helping to sort the crabs.

I set off down the bank at full speed, until I met the Welford family slowly carrying up their laden baskets and our Robbie trailing alongside them.

Hannah stopped as soon as she saw me. "What is it, honey?"

She spoke unusually kind as though she could see at once that I was frightened sick.

"Mam. She's fallen over and cracked our dolly tub."

"Why, never mind, lass, we'll find her another."

"Nay, nay. She cannot get up. She cannot even speak, and her face has . . . has shrunk to one side and it's horrible."

Hannah thrust her basket into the arms of her daughter, Mary. Then she took hold of me and held my hands tight to make me listen well.

"Now, honey, you must be brave for your mam. Run straight down to Miriam's and bring her quick. I shall go on up to help poor Annie. Come along with me, Robbie, don't look so fearful, lad, we'll see what we can do."

Old Miriam had been midwife, nurse and layer-out to the whole of Sandwick Bay since Mam were a little lass. It was not long before I was puffing back up the narrow cobbled path with Miriam puffing even harder beside me, clutching her basket of herbs and simples.

"Here, carry my medicines, lass," she gasped. "I swear I get too old for this."

Chapter 3

But Miriam was not too old for, skinny and bent though she was, she took us in hand and sorted us out before night came. With her help and Hannah's, we got the floor wiped clean and dry and the broken pot taken out to the back. We tucked Mam up in the bedplace downstairs by the kitchen fire.

Martha Welford and her daughter, Liza, brought us a supper of fresh boiled crabmeat and bread and milk. Liza bullied my brothers and sisters up to their beds and settled them all to sleep. She's a clever big girl is Liza and Miss Hindmarch has made her pupil teacher at our school, so we're all well used to doing as Liza Welford tells us.

Miriam patiently fed our mam with spoonfuls of a sleeping draught, and at last she slept, though her face and body still looked all wrong to me. I sat quietly by the fire watching her, while Miram settled herself in Mam's wooden rocking chair. It seemed she'd be staying the night.

"Miriam," I whispered at last. "Will she die?"

Miriam shook her head firmly.

"Will she mend then?"

Miriam frowned, shaking her head again. "That I can't say. I've seen it before, honey, and sometimes they mend and sometimes they don't."

I sat there in silence staring into the fire and worrying.

"Now, Dorothy," said Miriam. "Do you remember old Jimmy Loftus who died last spring? Remember how he dragged his left leg just a little?"

"Aye?"

"Well, he was same as your mam is now, and he got better

fine and lived on for years, and he was a worker, was Jimmy. You'd never have guessed there'd been anything wrong, just that little drag to the leg gave it away. Nowt to speak of."

"I pray my mam will be like him," I whispered.

Miriam rocked gently in Mam's chair.

"Aye," she nodded. "We'll both pray for that."

I crept up to the loft and climbed into bed beside Alice, and at last I slept. Having Miriam downstairs made me feel safe, despite our trouble.

Next morning I woke quite happy, thinking that it must have been a bad dream, but when I heard Miriam calling up our stairs for me, I knew that it was true and the fright came thundering back. I went down to find a grand breakfast of fried fishcakes waiting for us. Hannah had sent them round.

After we'd eaten, Hannah and Mary came to help us with the bairns, then Miriam told our Rob to take the little ones down to play on the staithe.

"I want to be here to help my mam," Rob said.

"Best way to help her is to give her peace and see to the bairns," Hannah insisted.

Rob sighed, but he did as she asked. I knew he'd rather be doing anything than watching his little brother and sisters.

I could see that all three women were tight-lipped and worried.

"Now we shall have to have a good talk," Miriam said.

"I think Dory should stay," said Mary, putting her arm about my shoulders. "She's a big enough lass and it is her right."

"I want to stay too," said Alice, her thin face all white and drawn.

Miriam nodded and I was glad. I crouched down beside my mam and stroked her hair. Alice came and sat close to me. She pushed her arm through mine, and for once I was really glad of her bony body pressing into my side.

17

Mam was awake and taking notice of all that went on, though she still could not speak. It was as though all the right side of her body had fallen asleep and would not move or work; not her arm, not her hand, not her leg.

Hannah sat down on the floor to speak to her.

"Annie," she said. "We are going to have to send to Whitby for the doctor."

"Naaah, naaah!" Mam struggled to make them understand.

Miriam bent forwards. "You must be calm, Annie, or you shall make yoursen worse. 'Tis bad, what's happened to you, and I cannot put you right, but maybe the Whitby doctor can do something. We cannot know unless he come and look at you."

It was then that I whispered aloud the thing that I knew must be troubling Mam.

"We've got no money to pay him with."

"Aye," Miriam sighed. "We shall have to apply to the Guardians. I fear there's no other way."

"But will they not send us to the workhouse?"

Mam lay quiet and helpless beside me, a tear trickled over her cheek.

"Not if we can help it," said Hannah. She bent down and took tight hold of Mam's hand. "I promise you this, Annie Lythe, we shall do all we can to keep you here in Sandwick Bay."

The Doctor came that afternoon in his pony and trap, and we were all sent outside. The little ones ran down to the crab boiling pots, happy enough for the moment, not understanding as Rob and Alice and I did that if the Whitby doctor came to call it must be bad.

We trailed slowly down the bankside after them, and found them greedily poking fresh crab meat from the claws they'd been given.

Nelly Wright was stirring the boiling tubs, her fat face red and sweating.

"Here y'are, Alice," she shouted, "and you, Dory . . . tek it then!"

Nelly, who's usually rude to everyone, was trying in her awkward way to be kind to us; thrusting steaming crabs' claws into our faces. I took it, but I'd little stomach for it. I could see sorrow in every face that turned our way. Folk smiled sadly at us, then looked away. It was clear enough; they wondered if we'd be in the workhouse within a week. I couldn't stand their pity.

"Keep your eye on the bairns," I told Alice sharply, and before she'd a chance to complain I was running over the staithe to the beach.

I marched furiously onwards, stamping through the shingle so that it crunched beneath my feet. A warm wind blew straight off the sea into my face, soothing me a little, but still I marched on and on towards the scaur. Then suddenly I stopped; two girls sat together on the big boat-shaped rock that we call Plosher Rock.

Though I wasn't close enough to see them clearly, I knew that it would be Liza Welford and Mary Jane Ruswarp. Best friends they'd always been, and they spent any free moment they had gossiping out there. I walked on, but slowly now, for they sat close together, very still. It was not like them to be so quiet. I almost forgot my own misery as curiosity gripped me.

At last they both turned at the sound of my footsteps in the shingle. I stopped then, ready to turn and run back to the staithe, feeling that I was nosing in on something private.

But Liza grinned and swung her legs round towards me.

"It's all right, Dory. We've got to be getting back. We've just been saying our goodbyes."

I looked from one to the other, wondering who was going.

I must have looked daft for they both laughed, and jumped down from the rock.

"Did you not know?" said Mary Jane. "This clever Miss Liza is going off to Whitby to play nursemaid to rich visitors."

Liza dug her elbow into Mary Jane's ribs. "She's such a jealous cat. I'm going to have a grand time. I'm to teach the children drawing and look after them, while their family's on holiday. I'm to have my own room in one of those huge smart houses, up on the West Cliff. Miss Hindmarch recommended me for the place."

"Oh, Liza," I whispered. "A room all to yourself? But Liza," I cried, my own fears crowding back in on me. "I might never see you again."

"'Course you will," Liza laughed, pushing her arm through mine. "I'll be back in the autumn for school."

"But we'll maybe not be here. Miriam says that they must apply to the Board of Guardians to pay Mam's doctor's bill, and I dread that they may send us all off to the Whitby Union Workhouse."

Liza stared at me, then looked over at Mary Jane. "Surely not?"

"Eeh dear, let's hope not," said Mary Jane, pushing her hand through my other arm.

They set off walking slowly back to the staithe, with me between them. I was cheered by their warmth; two big kind girls on either side of me, but they were both quiet.

"I doubt I'll bother going back to school," said Mary Jane. "Now that I'm fourteen I can work with my mam at the bait picking. I can't stay at school just to play on that organ."

"Take no notice of her! She'll be back at school!" Liza told me cheerfully. "Now that Miss Hindmarch is teaching her to play the hymns, you can't keep her away."

I smiled, for Mary Jane had amazed us all, and beneath her fingers the old school organ rippled into life.

"I love to hear you play," I told her.

"If there's just one thing I dream about," said Mary Jane,

"it'd be to have an organ at home. I can just see it standing there in mam's front room – but they cost so much."

When we reached the staithe, Mary Jane sighed and pulled a face at Liza. "Well, if Liza here is off to be a fine lady, there'll be nowt to do in Sandwick Bay. I might as well go off to Whitby myself for the herring gipping."

"What!" Liza exploded.

"Why not? I heard they'd such a good catch yesterday that they're asking for more girls. A lot of the Scotch girls have gone to Scarborough this year to suit the dealers."

"You?" Liza laughed. "They'd not have you! Gutting all that fish! It'd kill you!"

"I can gut fish . . . faster than you."

Liza grinned at her. "But not as fast as them."

"They get good money," said Mary Jane. "They get as much as a nursemaid. They get more if they're fast, and the catches are good."

"Aye, but look what they do for it." Liza shuddered and pinched her nose.

"I thought it was only the Scotch lasses that gipped the herrings," I said.

"Oh aye, it's mainly the Scotch lasses. They make it their living, those big tough girls. They manage to do it just about all year round. They get on the trains and off they go to wherever the fleet are."

"But where do they come from?" I asked.

"Oh, from way up north, and they get the trains right down to Lowestoft and Yarmouth in the autumn when the herrings swim south. Nobody can work like the Scotch lasses, but then, if the curers are short-handed in Whitby, they'll take on any woman that can do the gutting, just for the Whitby season. They'll not have trouble finding them for there's plenty round here that can gut fish, in't there? And plenty that want a bit of extra money."

"Would . . . would they take me on, d'you think? Maybe I could get some money for my mam?"

"Ey now, Dory," Liza hugged me. "The work they do is terrible. It'll surely not come to that."

Chapter 4

I walked over the staithe to where Alice and the little ones were playing hopscotch.

"We can take them back now," I told her. "The doctor must have had his say by now. Where's our Rob?"

She nodded her head, looking down to the sea where Rob was splashing through the shallows to help pull Dan Welford's coble up onto the beach.

"Leave him be," I said. "He'll come back when he's ready."

When we got back to Lythe's Yard, the doctor had gone and Miriam was busily whitening our front step.

"Ah, there you are," she looked up from her job. "I'm glad you're back. We've work to do."

"Please Miriam," I begged, "what has the doctor said?"

"Good news, I do believe. The doctor says he thinks your mam will recover in time, but listen well to this," she dropped her voice so that Mam shouldn't hear us. "The doctor says that she must not be vexed or fretful, that could make her worse."

I caught my breath. "But how can she not be fretful when she fears the workhouse so?"

"Aye, it's hard, honey, I know. But you two lasses can help a great deal by being brave and not fussing. Tomorrow they are sending the Reverend Hawkins down to see us and, as you know, he's on the Board of Guardians."

"Oh no," I cried.

Alice's face crumpled and her chin shook.

"Now, that's what I mean," Miriam told us. "It will fret

your mam to hear you weeping. We have to face up to this and all's not lost. Miss Hindmarch has sent to say that she'll come too. She knows the gentleman and she'll do her best to help. We must get this cottage spick and span so that the Reverend has nowt to complain about, and I shall offer to stay here with you to nurse your mam and see to the bairns. We must beg for just a few outside relief payments, to tide us over the worst."

I nodded my head, seeing the sense of that, though I knew that the Board of Guardians would not willingly give outdoor relief.

"Right," said Miriam. "We must set to. There's all this linen to press, then we've to parcel it up and deliver it. Alice, will you run and fetch your Rob? There's errands enough for him to do."

Rob came to help us willingly enough, and he ran up and down our bank with parcels of clean clothes, while we black-leaded our stove and polished till it gleamed. I tried to tell him what we planned and how we meant to keep us all together with Miriam's help, but he looked miserable.

"'Tis the only thing we can hope for," I told him.

"If I had a boat," he said, kicking the heavy iron mangle that stood in the corner of our yard, "then I could be a fisherman, and I could keep us all."

"Maybe one day, Robbie," I said, for I wished the same. "I'd fetch your bait, Robbie, and I'd clean your lines, but we've no boat and dreaming won't help us. So leave that mangle be . . . I fear we'll be needing it."

Alice and me lay awake that night, curled comfortably together for once.

"Oh, Dory," she whispered. "They say that they make you strip naked and they scrub you down with nasty smelling stuff and they cut off your hair."

"Hush," I tried to soothe her. "Maybe it's not as bad as people say."

"But they make you wear tight scratchy uniforms, I know that's true, for Johnny Liverton's grandpa were born in the workhouse, and he stayed there while he were a bairn. They take the babbies from the mams, and they take the lads from the lasses. Oh, Dory, we might never see our Robbie or Jackie again! Would we be put with the twins, do you think? Would you and me be together?"

"Ssh. Don't fret so." I held her tight and stroked her hair. I never knew how much I loved my sister till then. "Hush now," I whispered. "We must not worry our mam."

We were woken next morning by a great knocking on our door. I stumbled sleepily down the loft stairs, wondering why our Rob had not answered the knock. He'd been sent to sleep downstairs in the bedplace now that we'd got Mam settled upstairs.

Miriam came out of Mam's bedroom, yawning and half asleep, in her long white nightgown and sleeping bonnet.

"Are yer there? Are yer up?" A loud voice called, and the knocking continued.

"Whatever's going on?" Miriam sounded quite cross and muddled. "I told young Robbie to wake me soon after dawn."

"I know that voice," I said, running to open the door. "It's Nelly Wright, I'm sure of it."

I'd guessed right. There was Nelly standing on our doorstep, smiling broadly, as though we should be pleased to see her. Almost as though we should be expecting her.

"I've just to let yer know as he's all right," she said. "He'll be back in October with his pay, so he says."

"Let us know what?" Miriam snapped. "Who shall be back?"

"Their young Robbie, of course," said Nelly.

"Where is he?" I asked. "He should be down here, ready to wake us and build up the fire."

Nelly laughed as if that were the greatest joke. "Where is he? He's halfway to Whitby by now. That's what I'm telling yer. I passed him on the road an hour since and he'd his pillowcase slung over his back, all stuffed with straw for bedding. He says he's taken half a loaf for his dinner and he's off to Whitby to go with the herring boats."

We just stood there open-mouthed, staring at each other, then our Alice started to sob.

"Hush," I said, remembering Mam. I clapped my hand over her mouth.

Miriam quickly came to her senses. "Why, you daft lass," she told Nelly. "Why did you not stop him and bring him back?"

"Well," Nelly shrugged her shoulders, puzzled by the fuss. "I thought it were his own business. He's big enough, in't he? How old is he?"

"He's only eleven," I said. "Though he's big for his age, like me."

"They tek 'em at eleven," said Nelly.

"Is that right?" I asked Miriam.

She sighed. "I believe they do, honey."

"He'll be all right," Nelly told us cheerfully. "And he seems bent on fetching yer some money. Well, I've given yer't message. It's nowt to do wi' me."

And Nelly went off down the street, carrying a heavy pitcher of milk that slopped a little as she swayed.

We stood at our doorway, staring after her. We could think of nothing to say.

Just as we were about to go back inside, a great commotion arose down at the bottom of the bank. It seemed the whole of the Welford family were coming marching up the street. I saw Liza dressed in her Sunday best and then I remembered that she was off to Whitby to be a nursemaid.

"Liza, Liza," I shouted, jumping down from our step and running to catch hold of her arm, "our Rob has taken himself off to Whitby. He says he's going on a herring boat."

"Oh never!" she cried.

"Bless the lad!" Dan Welford cried. "I'm sorry, lass, and I do blame myself. He's been trying hard to get me to take him on with us, for we go to join in the herringing tonight. I said he were to stay here to see to his mam. I should have known he'd not take no for an answer."

"It's not your fault, Mr Welford," I said. "You know our Robbie; he'll do nowt that he's told."

"We'd all have said the same to him," Miriam agreed. "Will he get taken on, do you think?"

Dan Welford scratched his head. "He might well. The catches are so good that they're all joining in. I'll keep a look out for him, young Dory. If he's in any trouble, I'll take him on my boat."

"We'd be much obliged," I said. Then I kissed Liza, and I wished her well.

"I'll see you in October," she told me firmly.

Chapter 5

The Reverend Hawkins and Miss Hindmarch sat at our kitchen table and sipped their tea from Hannah's best china cups. The gentleman was stout with a curling grey moustache. He wore a good black suit, and he'd put down his hat on Mam's rocking chair. Miss Hindmarch nodded smiles at him and us, and complimented Miriam on the cleanliness of the children and of the cottage.

Alice and I stood quietly side by side, our hands linked tightly together. The little ones shuffled impatiently, though I felt proud of the way that they looked; faces and hands scrubbed, their hair brushed neatly and aprons clean. Though Mam was settled in her bed upstairs, I knew she'd be lying awake, straining to catch what was said.

"Do you think perhaps the youngest children could be allowed to go outside now?" Miss Hindmarch asked the Reverend.

He nodded, and Miriam told Alice to take them out. I wanted to go running out with them down to the staithe, running away from all our troubles, but I knew that I had to stay.

There was a knock on the door and Hannah and Martha Welford both came in. They bowed their heads politely to the visitors.

The Reverend Hawkins looked a little surprised. "Relatives only," he said.

Hannah folded her arms and smiled. "Aye. We're all family in Sandwick Bay, sir."

Then our door opened quietly again and in stepped Mrs Ruswarp and old Mrs Wright and, though the clergyman looked puzzled, he didn't object again. After all, what Hannah said was true enough. Though we had no close family left, we had so many second and third cousins that we lost track of who was who.

At last the Reverend gentleman cleared his throat. He turned to Miriam. "What you propose, dear lady, is most generous, and if poor Mrs Lythe were likely to recover her health in a week or two, the Board of Guardians could make such outdoor relief payments. But let us face it, recovery could take months or even years. Mrs Lythe would get proper attention in the hospital wing of the workhouse and the children would be taught their manners and some useful work."

I clenched my hands together behind my back until they hurt, biting my lips to stop the tears from coming.

"I do assure you that they are all good mannered, hard-working children," Miss Hindmarch smiled sweetly at the man. "And they are so close to their mother since their father's death. Might it not seem a great charity to keep the family together?"

"Yes, yes," he nodded impatiently. "But you say the young boy has already gone off to Whitby."

"He's gone off to earn some money for the family," Miriam told the gentleman firmly. "Though we're fearful for him, being only eleven years old."

Reverend Hawkins shrugged his shoulders. "I should say that it's commendable in the child. If there were just a little more money coming in to the home. Some prospect of earnings . . ."

Suddenly he pointed his finger in my face. "How old are you child?"

I stammered with shock. "I . . . I'm thirteen . . . sir."

Miss Hindmarch was full of kind concern. "Dorothy's a good girl, but she's never been away from home."

My heart was thumping with fear. I could see the way

things were going; I was like to be sent away from home to work. The very thought terrified me, but if it would only keep Mam and the little ones safe here, then I knew I must do it.

"She's tall and she looks strong enough," the Reverend Hawkins insisted. "You say she's helped her mother with the washing. She could be found a place as a laundry maid. Then we might well be in a position to consider outdoor relief payments until her wages are sent home."

There was silence in our cramped little room. The women did not look at me. I knew they would not like the choices being offered, but they could see no way to help. I must go away and earn us some money, or we'd all be sent to the workhouse. But I was damned if I was going to be a laundry maid.

I had to gather together all the small courage that I'd got and, though my mam was brought so low that she could not speak to me, something that she'd often told me crept into my mind.

"Don't droop your head so, Dory," she'd say. "When you hold up your head and stand tall, there's no finer lass in all the Bay."

So I took a deep breath and I did it. I held up my head and looked straight at Reverend Hawkins, and I said,

"Not a laundry maid, sir. I shall go to be a herring gutter."

Again there was silence and everyone stared at me, but the clergyman smiled, and suddenly he seemed to find me most amusing. I was all muddled in my mind and could only think what strong white teeth he'd got.

"And what makes you think you'll be a herring girl and not a laundry maid?"

I knew the answer to that all right. "My father was a fisherman, sir."

Reverend Hawkins looked amazed, but a ripple of sighs came from the women. They understood.

I smiled. I suddenly knew how to please the man, so I

31

spoke again. "And another thing, sir, a herring girl earns more money if she's fast."

He laughed at that, while the women shuffled and whispered together behind me.

"A herring girl must certainly be fast! Are you fast?"

My usual fear and shyness came flooding back.

"I . . . I will learn to be, sir."

But Miriam came to stand by me then, snatching up my hand in hers. I think she knew that my courage had ebbed away as fast as it came.

"'Tis terrible hard work for a little lass, but if Dorothy feels that she can do it, then I can certainly see to the bairns and nurse her mother while she's away."

Miss Hindmarch looked worried at the way things were going, but the vicar turned to her shaking his head.

"It's quite ridiculous! Good-mannered did you say? The girl must be a laundry maid. It's what she's been taught."

My heart sank heavy as ironstone.

But then Hannah came to stand on the other side of me.

"The girl can gut fish," she said. "I've taught her that. You said yourself, sir, she's tall and strong."

"So I did, but, well, don't those women work in teams?"

"Aye, they do. But we shall find a team from the village. We can fix her up as one of three."

The Reverend Hawkins face grew serious. "Doesn't she need equipment, knives and such like?"

"We'll find her the knives that she needs." It was Martha Welford speaking now.

The man looked up at the women. Something had changed in our small kitchen. They'd gathered around me like a warm, strong blanket. They spoke as one, with stubborn determination. I'd seen it before, often enough. They'd gang up on a man who beat his wife, or strip the trousers from a lad who courted too freely. I could not believe it, for though they must think I'd gone barmy, still they stood by me.

32

Hannah spoke for them all.

"If the child can face the hard work, then we shall find all that she needs."

It wasn't till the visitors had gone that it really hit me, and I realised what I'd let myself in for. I started shaking all over so that Miriam made me sit by the fire and sip some hot sweet tea.

The women didn't fuss me.

"Aye, she's bound to feel like that," said Hannah, in her matter-of-fact way. "You can sit for a bit, Dory, but you can't sit for long; there's much to do. I shall go straight down to the staithe to speak to our Frank. He and Dan are making the plosher ready for the herringing."

"Right," said Martha. "See if they'll hold back a hundred herrings, for we'll have to teach her to gip."

"But I can gut a cod or a haddock," I said, quite offended. "Didn't Aunt Hannah tell the gentleman that I could?"

"Never mind what I told him!" said Hannah. "Gipping a herring is quite a different matter, and I shall have told no lie, for I will teach you to gip before you go to Whitby, and you are going to have to learn fast, my girl."

"We'll send a message to Cousin Rachel," said Martha. "She sometimes lets her rooms to herring girls. She used to be fond of Annie, when we were lasses. She'd help you out, Dory, and keep a bit of an eye on you."

"That's a grand idea," Hannah agreed. "But first things first. Finding a team of three is the sticky thing. 'Twould be best if we could find someone who's done it before. Your Irene would be good, but I doubt if she'd leave that bairn."

Martha shook her head. "I'd have the little lad, quick as a flash, she knows that, but she's besotted with the bairn."

I got up from the fireside, for I'd my own ideas about who might make up the team, and I knew I must get busy before I got too scared and changed my mind.

"I think I might know someone who'd go wi' me."

"Our Nelly might," said old Mrs Wright as she set off

home. "She were on about it the other night. I'll speak to her."

I said nothing till she and Mrs Ruswarp had gone, but I wasn't keen on going off to Whitby with their Nelly. Miriam's sharp eyes caught the look on my face.

"You could do worse than Nelly," she told me. "I seem to recall that Nelly's done the gipping once before, and again it were illness that caused it. Her father was laid up one summer with a bad leg, and old Mrs Wright took Nelly off to Whitby with her. They worked all through the season, and Nelly can't have been older than you are now, Dory. She's a tough 'un, is that Nelly, and that's what you want."

Chapter 6

I scooted down the bank as fast as I could, looking for Mary Jane, my whole body prickling with the excitement of it all. I hadn't said anything to Mrs Ruswarp about it for I didn't know what she'd think, Mary Jane being her youngest.

Alice was sitting on the staithe with our twins and Jackie. I knew I must tell her and not waste time.

"Well?" she cried. "What have they said?"

"We're not to go in the workhouse so you can stop worrying about that. I'm to go off to Whitby to gip the herrings and earn us some money."

"Oh no, Dory, no. You cannot do that. Not you and Robbie both gone."

"Now stop that," I wagged a finger in her face. "I'll be back when the herrings swim south in October, and Miriam will look after you till then."

"I don't like Miriam," she said, her chin trembling. "She's old and snappy."

I sighed and I put my arms about her. "Come on, Alice. You've to be the big lass now."

"I'm our big boy," little Jackie spoke up cheerfully, catching what we said. "I'm our big boy now Robbie's gone."

"Aye," I said, and I reached out and slapped his rump to tease him. "You're the big boy. Tell our Alice that she must be the big girl."

"Big girl," he said giggling, and thumped Alice on the head.

"Big girl, big girl," the twins echoed.

I turned serious, "It's either Miriam or the workhouse. Which do you want Alice?"

A faint smile touched her lips. "If that's what I've got to choose, then I want Miriam," she whispered.

There was no sign of Mary Jane on the staithe or in the yards, and I was just wondering whether I'd have to go knocking on the Ruswarps' door when it came flooding into my mind that I knew exactly where she'd be.

I ran across the staithe and onto the sand. It was a hot afternoon, and the rocking of the waves sent glittering shots of sunlight into my eyes. I was dizzy with the regular swish and fizz of the sea, as it washed against the pebbles. The faster I tried to go, the more my feet seemed to sink into the soft dry sand. But Mary Jane was there, just where I thought she'd be; a small lonely figure sitting on Plosher Rock.

"Mary Jane! Mary Jane!" I yelled at her, waving my arms.

She looked up at once and stared at me, then she turned away disappointed. I swear she'd hoped for a moment that it was Liza Welford, come back to Sandwick Bay. I could see that she didn't feel much like bothering with me, but I'd no time for messing about.

"Please Mary Jane," I panted, crunching through the shingle, and throwing my arms over Plosher Rock. "Please Mary Jane, I'm begging you. Will you come with me to Whitby to gip the herrings?"

"What?" she stared at me amazed.

"Well, I am surely going," I told her. "It's all fixed. I've either to do that or go as a laundry maid, and I'd rather be a herring gutter. The Guardians will make outdoor relief payments for my mam if I go away to earn some money. So you see I've got to go, but now I must find myself two more to make a team of three, and fat Nelly might be one of them – but I hope not."

The words tumbled fast from my mouth; I couldn't stop to draw breath.

Mary Jane listened to it all in shocked silence.

"You must be mad," she said at last.

I waited by the rock, dismayed and miserable. I knew that I could not wait for long. If she would not come with me, I must get on and find another.

"Well," I said at last. "I thought I'd ask, after what you said yesterday. I daresay you were only teasing Liza, and never meant it. You've no need to earn money, not like me."

I turned to go, and started back across the shingle.

"Wait!" Mary Jane called after me. She swung herself down from the rock, and ran to push her arm through mine. "Wait a while. I do want money! I was only teasing yesterday, but now you've made me wonder. Do you think I'd earn enough to buy an organ?"

I smiled. "If the catches are good, and we can work fast enough, then I think you might."

"I'll be miserable here in Sandwick without Liza, and now you're going too, Dory. At least it's all go in Whitby, though I swear the work will kill us."

"I daren't even think about it," I told her. "I've just got to do it."

"Well," said Mary Jane. "We'd better find another to make up our team, and not Nelly Wright."

"You'll come then?"

"I must be mad! But I'll come with you. I'd best go to tell my mam."

Mrs Ruswarp frowned at us both, and then she sighed, but she accepted it.

"You both seem such little lasses to be going off to work like this. Still, I know that you must go, Dory love, and most folk would think that Mary Jane is quite old enough at fourteen. It's just that she's my baby, you see."

Mary Jane kissed her mam. "Wait till you see the money I'll fetch back wi' me. And Mam, how would you like to see a beautiful polished wood organ standing in your parlour?

Mrs Ruswarp smiled and shook her head. "Just see that you find an older body for the third."

We went knocking on the Welfords' door to see Irene. We didn't hold out much hope of her coming, but we thought she'd be the best one to ask; her being kind, and having done the gutting before.

"I thought she'd maybe need a bit of money for the bairn," I whispered to Mary Jane, but she shook her head.

"You know their Frank? The one that went fighting in the war? Well, he's got himself a job up at Stockton now, working in the steelworks. He sends Irene money to help her with the lad. Our John were his friend you know."

I nodded silently, sorry that I'd reminded Mary Jane of her drowned brother John.

Irene opened the door with little Joby in her arms.

"I know what you want, Dory, but this bairn's right fretful and awake all night. He's starting cutting his teeth, so that I can't bear to leave him with my mam."

Joby smiled at us, and dribbled.

"Give your auntie a kiss," Mary Jane insisted, smacking her lips at Joby till he giggled.

Joby's father, John Ruswarp, had been Mary Jane's eldest brother, but John had died before ever Joby was born. All the village treasured the baby, for none of them could ever forget the fierce storm that had drowned his father, and the terrible struggle that they'd had to save the other men.

Irene had had a hard time getting through her pregnancy, she'd been so sick and so miserable. But then when Joby was born, she'd not stayed sad for long, for you'd never seen a bairn with a happier, funnier face. Just one look at him and you had to smile, whether you wished to or not. Irene had named him John, for his father, but the villagers had insisted on calling him John's boy, and after a while it had shortened itself to Joby.

"I don't blame you for not wanting to leave him," I told

Irene. "I'd not want to leave him either. Mary Jane is going to come with me."

"Eeh dear! I hope you both know what you're taking on," she said. "I've got something for you, though. I've gipping knives and a good wooden trunk. Come on in and have a look!"

The trunk was a proper kist box, the kind that the Scotch girls used, with its wooden shottle drawer at the top, made specially to hold the knives, and space beneath for clothes.

"I'd think you two could share one box," said Irene. "It's not as though you're going right down to Yarmouth, like the Scotch girls do."

I agreed with that for the trunk looked big to me, and I'd nothing to put in it. I'd only my best clothes and my working clothes and that was it.

We carried the kist box round to the Ruswarps' cottage, and then we went banging on the Pickerings' door.

Bessie Pickering was one of the younger married women who'd got no children. She smiled when she saw us and asked us in. It seemed the whole village knew our business.

"I do wish you well," she said. "I was meaning to help with the gipping this year, but I've just come to realise that I'm expecting. I've wanted a bairn for more than three years now, so I'll not take any risks."

We said that we were pleased for her, and we were just about to go when she lifted a great pile of cotton strips down from her sideboard.

"I've been saving flour bags all through the winter," she said. "I've cut them into bandage strips. You'll be needing them now, instead of me."

I remembered then how the herring girls must bandage up their thumbs and their first two fingers to save them from the cuts. We took the cotton strips most gratefully.

Though we knocked on doors all through the afternoon, we could not find a woman who was willing and free to

come gipping with us. Still, we didn't come away empty handed. We were given strong oilskin aprons, with straps that crossed at the back, old working skirts and shirts, and worn-out knitted ganseys that the fishermen wore to keep them from freezing out on the sea. There was a pot of Mrs Love's ointment for curing cuts, and a deal of sound advice to go with it.

Mary Jane and I were worn out when we got back to the Ruswarps' cottage, our arms piled high with gifts.

"Mam! You should see what we've been given," Mary Jane called out. "But we've still got nobody to make a third."

Mrs Ruswarp nodded her head towards their kitchen. There standing in front of their fire place was Nelly Wright.

"Yer should have asked me," Nelly said. "I'll come to Whitby wi' yer. There y'are then . . . that's all right."

Chapter 7

It was quiet back at the cottage. Miriam had sent the three younger children off to bed and she and Alice were ironing our Sunday-best clothes. Buckets of washing were soaking out in the yard.

"More washing?" I said. I wanted to cry when I saw those buckets. "They'll keep on sending it, won't they? What shall we do? And why have you ironed our Sunday clothes?"

Miriam smiled and shook her head. "Don't you always press your clothes on Saturday night?"

"It can't be Saturday already," I said.

So much had happened that I'd got my days all muddled.

"Stop fussing, Dory," said Alice, suddenly all grown-up. "This is our washing. We've not had much chance to deal with it, so we've set it to soak till Monday. Miriam has sent messages telling our customers that Mam is sick and cannot take in washing for a while."

"Oh thank you, Miriam," I said, relieved. Suddenly I was blinking back tears. "You're doing that much to help us and I can't see as we can ever repay it."

Miriam waved her hands in the air. "Now Dory, you know that I never had bairns of my own so I'm glad o' the chance to see to other folks little 'uns."

I nodded my head and wiped my eyes.

"Mam's wanting you," Alice told me. "She's made it plain enough."

"What shall I say to her?" I looked at Miriam.

"Say nowt," Miriam shrugged her shoulders. "I've told her that you're off to Whitby. I don't think she likes it much, but she can still think straight; she knows there's little choice. Now up you go, she wants to see you."

Mam was propped up on the pillows. Miriam had left an oil lamp burning low on the small cupboard beside her, so that Mam's silver hairs glowed golden against the brown ones. She looked a bit better to me.

"Oh, Mam," I said, and I went to put my arms about her. We stayed like that for a moment my cheek against hers; she stroked my hair with her good hand. But then she pulled away.

"What is it?" I asked.

"Naah . . . naah!" Mam pointed down towards the bottom of the bed.

"What is it you want?" I asked stupidly. "A rug? A drink? Miriam?"

"Naah . . . naah." She tried again, and I carefully followed where she pointed.

"Dad's sea chest?"

She nodded at last, and beckoned me to bring it to her.

I grabbed the handle of the heavy chest and dragged it across the room. I lifted the lid with shaking hands. Most times Mam would not let us touch it, though we knew well what was inside. We treated those few poor things with reverence: Dad's old clothes, his Sunday-best suit, his three clay pipes all different sizes and his bowler hat.

Mam lurched to the side of the bed, trying to reach down into the trunk.

"What is it?" I asked again.

Mam couldn't seem to find what she wanted. She waved her good hand wildly in the air.

"Naah! Naah," she cried out with rage. I was feared to see her so vexed and helpless.

"Whatever is wrong?" Miriam appeared at the top of our narrow stairs.

"I do believe she wants me to tip Dad's sea chest out."

"Well, in that case, I should do it, honey."

So I did, I tipped all my father's things so that they rolled out onto the bedroom floor. Mam calmed down straight away; she went quiet and thoughtful, inspecting the stuff carefully, then at last she pointed clearly at his boots.

"Dad's sea boots?"

Mam nodded, and I picked them up. They were his best pair and they were almost unworn.

"What am I to do with them?" I looked at Miriam, puzzled.

"You're to wear them, Dory, what do y'think?" Miriam chuckled and Mam pointed to my feet.

"I'm to wear my dad's best boots?" I whispered.

"I think your mam wants that," said Miriam. "There's nowt better. You've to stand for hours in the muck and wet, and they'll keep you comfortable and dry. There's many a herring girl wears her dad's old sea boots. You're to have a strong decent pair that's hardly worn."

I shook my head. "They're too big."

It wasn't really the size that troubled me, more that it seemed a sinful thing to wear my poor dead father's boots.

"They won't be," Miriam said firmly. "Not when you've three pair o' woolly socks inside 'em."

I looked at Mam, and I could see that she tried to smile though it came out all lopsided. A tear ran down her cheek.

"Oh thank you, Mam," I said, hugging the boots to my chest. "I'll take good care o' them and clean them well. Now I've summat precious to put in Irene's trunk."

Miriam made us go to Sunday school, as we usually did, and I sat quietly with Mam all Sunday afternoon.

On Monday I woke early and I dressed and went straight round to Hannah's cottage, for Hannah had promised to teach us how to gip herrings. Mary Jane was there, all sleepy and yawning.

"Is Nelly learning to gip?" I asked.

"She is not." Mary Jane giggled. "Fastest herring gipper in Sandwick is Nelly . . . or so she says."

44

We'd got three baskets with two hundred overday herrings that Frank and Dan Welford had kept back from the dealers on Saturday, so that we could practise our gipping. It was good of them, for decent-sized herrings were selling for three shilling a hundred in Whitby.

"They've landed six lasts in Whitby this week," said Hannah.

We were impressed at that, for it meant more than sixty thousand herrings caught in just a few days' work.

"And they're expecting more Cornishmen to arrive tonight. It's just like the old days. Fancy them Cornishmen sticking to fishing out of Whitby, when so many dealers have gone over to Scarborough."

"Why is Scarborough so favoured now?" I asked.

"The dealers are asking for new building work to be done on Whitby harbour, but the Board hasn't the money." Hannah shrugged her shoulders. "So it's loyal of these Cornish chaps to stick with us. My Frank says Whitby's the place for Penzancemen, no matter what. They like the chapels, see."

"Has Mr Welford seen owt of our Robbie?" I begged.

Hannah shook her head. "I'm sorry, lass, but they'll be looking again today, and you must seek for him yourself. I've asked our Frank and Dan to take you lasses round to Whitby tonight?"

"What?" said Mary Jane. "We've not even learnt how to gut a herring yet!"

"You'll either've learnt by tonight or never," said Hannah. "They're telling me the curers have fixed up three teams of Whitby women. Either you go tonight or you'll have missed your chance. Our cousin, Rachel Welford, has sent to say that she's getting her downstairs room ready for you. She'll see you're all right."

Mary Jane pulled a face, and whispered in my ear. "Aye. She'll see us all right. Just like Hannah, she is."

"What's that?" said Hannah. "No time for fooling, Mary

Jane, you fetch those gipping knives and those oilie aprons. We must get on."

"Oilie aprons? While we're learning?" Mary Jane looked amazed.

"Aye . . . aprons, boots and bandages. You're like to make a worse mess now than ever, and you don't want to start it all with a bad cut. Come on! Fetch all the stuff! Spread that oilskin on my table top!"

Hannah made us bandage up our fingers carefully, and tie the knots with our teeth for, as she said, there'd be nobody to help us in Whitby, and no time to help each other. I knew then what a grand present Bessie had made us, for we'd never have been able to find the stuff and carefully cut up all those bandages ourselves.

My first attempts at gipping were useless.

"Nay, Dory, lass," Hannah cried. "You're bringing out good flesh. Here let me stand behind you. Start slow and get it right! You'll come into speed later.

I gripped the plump silver-skinned fish and Hannah put her hand over mine to guide the short sharp gipping knife.

"There now, make the cut in its throat like that, then push in so. Now a quick twist to pick up the guts, then gently flick – and out they come."

The strong smelling herring guts slopped out onto the oilskin cover.

"Is that it?" I asked. The fish stared mournfully up at me, its eyes still bright on either side of its upturned nose. It looked almost untouched, just a small neat hole in its throat.

"That's it," said Hannah. "So long as the gut and the gills are out. Now try yourself."

I copied her carefully, trying to judge the right spot to push in my knife, and just the right angle to pick up the guts when I twisted. And I did judge it right, but I pulled the knife out fast and a slimy spurt of fish guts shot up into my face. The stinking guts went up my nose, and into my mouth.

Hannah snorted with laughter and Mary Jane shrieked out loud. I staggered back, spluttering and spitting. The herring guts tasted foul.

"Ugh! Dory," yelled Mary Jane.

"Eeeh! Dory love," cried Hannah. "I know it's wicked to laugh. But . . . oh, your face! The guts should go in the gut tub, honey! There's a cloth behind you. Now then, come on, we'll try again."

I wiped my face and shuddered, I couldn't stop spitting.

"It's all right you laughing," I told Mary Jane. "I've not seen you bring the guts out yet."

We worked slowly all morning under Hannah's instruction, and when we'd used up almost thirty herrings, we'd begun to get the knack of hitting the right spot and bringing the guts out each time. Our arms and aprons were spattered with mess and our bandaged fingers slippery and wet, but Hannah had made us work slowly and we'd not cut ourselves.

Hannah set three baskets behind us and showed us how to judge the size of each herring, and throw the gutted fish carefully into the right basket. The smallest ones were called Matties. The medium-sized fish were called Mattiefulls, and the largest herrings were called Fulls. Hannah made us guess the size and shout it out as we gutted. If we guessed wrong, she scooped the fish out and made us do it all again. At noon she let us stop.

"I'll make us a pot of tea," she said. "Though there'll be no stopping for breaks in Whitby you know."

Mary Jane slumped down onto a chair.

"Mind my decent furniture with those filthy oilies!" Hannah snapped. "You can sit on the doorstep if you must."

We sat on Hannah's doorstep and sipped our tea. Apart from the gentle babble of Alice and the bairns next door, the village seemed deserted. I frowned. Where had they all gone? Then suddenly it came to me.

"Is it Regatta Day?" I asked.

"Why, you great daft head," Mary Jane laughed. "O' course it's Regatta Day. You must be flummoxed with all your troubles, Dory."

I nodded, and I turned to Hannah, who sat on her chair behind us. "You've missed Whitby Regatta to teach us how to gip."

Hannah smiled kindly and shook her head.

"I've seen plenty of regattas, honey, and I daresay I'll see plenty more."

Mary Jane groaned, and rolled her shoulders back.

"I'm aching already," she said. "We must be mad! Why are we doing it?"

"Money," I answered her quickly. "Think of that fine organ standing in your mam's best room."

I didn't need to remind myself how badly that money was needed.

Chapter 8

The two Welford brothers had to row hard for the tide was against them. I clutched tight to the side of their plosher that was named the *Esther Welford*. She was one of the big five-man coble boats that the Whitby men use for chasing the herring. They'd had to come away from the regatta early, in order to row us back to Whitby before the herring fleet went off for the night.

The afternoon had passed in a whirl of fast fish gutting, and then frantic last minute packing of Irene's trunk.

I was all of a dither, and I think Mary Jane was worn out and regretting her promise to come to Whitby and work. Nelly had come up to Hannah's to watch us gip.

"Yer'll have t'work faster 'n that," she told us. "Ey dear, I can see as I'm going to be having to do most of t' gipping. You two'll have to take turns at packing."

"I shouldn't think they'll complain at that," Hannah said.

"You don't have to come with us, Nelly," Mary Jane said, hopefully.

"I'll put up wi'yer," said Nelly. "I've got me box ready now."

We'd been so busy that I couldn't think straight. I hadn't said goodbye to my mam or to Alice. It was Miriam who'd come down to the staithe and kissed me. Our Jackie and little Nan and Polly had been there waving, all cheerful and excited. I don't think they realised that they'd not be seeing me again for two months. They thought I was having a nice ride in the Welfords' plosher.

Nelly sat beside me, smiling calmly as the big coble pulled

49

out of the bay, taking it all in her stride. She was twenty-one and she was a big woman. One of the few older lasses who'd no young man to court her. I'd always been wary of her; she'd tease the bairns and she could be right rough and loud-mouthed. You never quite knew what she'd do or what she'd say.

Mary Jane sat in the stern along with her brother, Sam, who often worked the boat with the Welford brothers. She was telling him that she'd have finished his gansey by the time the herring season was over.

"You ought to knit a gansey, Dory," she told me. "All the herring lasses knit ganseys."

Knitting the warm jumpers that we call ganseys is vital work for all fishermans' wives and daughters. There's never an excuse for idle hands in our small village and the women are knitting away every spare minute of the day. Without their fine ganseys to keep out the wet and cold, our men would freeze out on the sea.

I shrugged my shoulders. "Who should I knit for?" I asked.

"Your Robbie of course; he's a fisherman now, in't he?"

"Aye, maybe," I answered. "But if I find him safe, I'll send him home."

Nelly laughed and shook her head. "He'll not go," she told me. "He'll not tek notice of his sister fussing at 'im. Not that lad. He were that determined when he spoke to me."

I sighed. "If he'll not go home, then I'll knit him a gansey."

We fell quiet as we left our bay. My stomach lurched as the boat rolled with the waves. In the distance, we could see the fleet of visiting herring boats riding at anchor in the sea roads off Whitby harbour.

I smiled to myself. I remembered the delicious smell of fried herrings that had come to us as we carried our boxes down to the staithe. We'd laughed about it. The smell seemed to waft from every window and every doorway. The whole of Sandwick Bay had come back from Whitby Regatta, full of excitement at who'd won the coble race and who'd won the long boat race, to find they'd cheap fresh herrings for their tea. Hannah had sent our Jackie and Billy Welford round the houses selling the herrings that we'd gutted at a halfpenny a pair.

The sea grew choppy, and the sky darkened as though we might be in for rain.

"We're going a long way out," I said, trying not to sound worried.

I'd not had much chance to go out in the boats since Dad died.

"Don't fret, young Dory," Dan Welford winked at me. "We have to follow the sea roads, so we don't catch the scaur. They're right awkward are those low lying rocks. They stretch for more than a mile, so we must go out further, just to keep ourselves clear of them."

"I'd not want to do this every day," I said. "Our Robbie must be daft.

"Aye, we're all daft," Frank Welford said cheerfully. "And your Robbie's another stubborn fellow, just like his father."

There were spots of rain and the boat rocked wildly as we drew close to the Cornish boats with their double masts and lug sails. I was feeling very sick, and wondering what the men'd say if I begged them to take me back to the bay, when they turned the boat southerly to ride with the tide and we could see Whitby harbour small and flat looking and misty in the distance.

We went towards it fast then; my stomach pulling itself tight with excitement. My spirits lifted with the boat as it rode the waves towards the town.

As soon as we passed through the curved arms of the harbour, the sea grew calm, and Whitby seemed to rear itself high about us on either side of the river Esk.

51

Smoke from the chimneys mingled with the mist.

"Oh, look at the Abbey," I shrieked at Mary Jane. "And St Mary's church up on the clifftop, and all those grey stone stairs."

"Henrietta Street," she shouted, pointing wildly at the old street that ran below St Mary's church. The small houses up there seemed lost in clouds of puthering smoke. "See, it's got the little beach below it. That's where we're stopping."

"I don't know what yer both yelling about," said Nelly. "This here's the fish quay where yer'll be working. And yer'd better get used to the smell of bloaters and red herrings, for Henrietta Street's nowt but smoke-houses."

Cousin Rachel was waiting for us by the fish quay on Pier Road. There were no herring girls in their usual places that day as all the work had stopped for the regatta.

Rachel was a small woman, about Mam's age, with grey hair combed smooth beneath the blue cotton bonnet that all the fisherwomen wore in the summer months. She stood by the harbour rail, her arms folded over the top of a spotless white apron. She had that stony, determined look that I knew well. Most of the fishwives had that same look. You'd have a job to pull the wool over their eyes.

She gave Mary Jane a quick kiss and turned to me.

"So you're Annie Lythe's oldest lass. I knew your mam when we were young. You've more a look of your father though. Now then, Nelly! I spoke to the curer's chaps this morning and told them you were on your way, but they've fixed up two more teams and they say they don't need any more."

"You mean we're too late?" Mary Jane looked horrified.

I couldn't bear the thought of going back to Sandwick Bay empty-handed now that we were here in Whitby.

"Can we not ask again?" I tried to make my voice sound calm, though I was desperate inside.

"'Course we can," Nelly told me. "Yer can't expect to be taken on just like that."

"Oh aye. We must ask again tomorrow, honey," Rachel said kindly. "No need to give up yet. I've heard all about your mam, and I know you need the work. The room's all cleared and ready for you, so come on back to Henrietta Street and I'll make you a bit of tea."

We said our goodbyes to Dan and Frank, but I kept staring at the big wooden farlanes that the coopers were setting up on Pier Road, ready for the herring girls in the morning.

"Come on," Nelly said. "Never mind gawping at them, time for that tomorrow. Tek up my box, will yer! Rachel and Mary Jane have taken yours."

"Can yer not hold it up a bit," Nelly complained as we followed the others over the bridge.

I'd remembered that I should be looking out for our Robbie, and what with that and the busy streets my head turned this way and that. We went down Sandgate, and up through the market place, and along Church Street. It was full of the whirring of machines and tapping sounds that came from the busy jet workshops.

"They're doing all right," Rachel told us. "Ever since the old Queen lost her husband and took to wearing the black jet stones in her jewellery, business has been booming."

We reached the bottom of Abbey stairs and went past them into Henrietta Street.

"Eeh, you can smell bloaters up here." I laughed, my eyes watering a little.

"You'll soon get used to it," Rachel said. "Mr Fortune's sheds are up on the bankside, just opposite my bedroom window. I only ever take notice if he's not got fish smoking for some reason."

Nelly's box was heavy and I was ready to drop it when Rachel stopped to open her front door. It was one of the last few cottages on the harbour side of the street, though the pathway carried on past more smoke-houses and led down to the East Pier.

The door next to Rachel's opened and a woman stuck her head out; another fisherman's wife, by her bonnet and apron. She looked at our boxes, surprised.

"Now Rachel, what's this? I thought you weren't taking Scotch lasses this year."

"I'm not," said Rachel. "This lot's from Sandwick. You've seen Mary Jane before, and this'n's Annie Lythe's lass, and this'n's Nelly."

"Have they fixed them up, then?"

"No," said Rachel. "They'll have to try again in the morning."

The woman clicked her tongue and shut her door.

"That's my neighbour, Hannah Smith," Rachel told us. "She's known as Trickey around here. You can guess why! She's a good enough neighbour to me though. She's got eight of the Scotch girls stopping with her. You'll hear them when they come back."

I stared at Trickey's door. Eight Scotch girls? Where did she put them all. The cottages were bigger than ours in Sandwick, but they weren't that big.

Rachel went into a narrow passage with a door to the right. She flung it open, and we saw a small bare basement room with three steps down to it.

"There you are," Rachel said. "I've put you in here so that you don't need to traipse through the rest of the house."

Nelly and I followed the others in, bumping her box down the three steps.

The room was so dark and dismal that my spirits sank. It was all so very bare, nothing in but three beds, covered with worn patchwork quilts. Our living rooms at Sandwick bloomed with fine brass ornaments and pictures and I'd expected the same. In Rachel's room the floorboards were covered with oilcloth, and the curtains that hung at the window, just above the street level, had brown paper pinned carefully over them. There were no curtains at all on the far small window that overlooked the harbour and beach.

"I've had a good clear-out, as you can see," Rachel told us, as though we should be pleased. "So now you won't need to worry about mess."

"Aye," said Nelly. "I prefer it like that," and she thumped herself down on the bed nearest to the street window.

"I'll make some tea, and give you a shout," said Rachel. "You can come up to my kitchen today, but once you're working I'll bring your food and drink to you. I'll want your boots and oilies left outside of course."

The three of us were left together. Nelly swung her legs up onto her bed, trying it and prodding it.

"Not bad," she decided.

Mary Jane looked across at me. I think she felt a bit lost too.

"I knew they cleared the best furniture out," she said. "I just didn't think how plain it'd leave it. We haven't even a chair to sit on."

"We sit on't boxes, of course!" Nelly said, disgusted at our ignorance.

I went to peep out of the window on the harbour side, and I got a grand view of the West Cliff and the boats in the harbour, making ready to set off for the night.

"Can I have this bed?" I asked, going to the nearest one.

"You can," said Nelly. "I'm not sleeping there. I don't want the sea keeping me awake all night."

Chapter 9

Rachel called us up to her kitchen and I was glad to see that it was as bright and cosy as any in Sandwick Bay. She served thick slices of bread with a little butter and sweet bilberry jam.

"The bairns fetch t' berries down from the moors," she told us. "Then they come round knocking on doors with their hands and faces stained black and purple. They've the cheek to ask a penny a basket, but they're fine berries for jam, and my husband has a sweet tooth, so I usually buy from them."

The food cheered me for a moment. It looked as though we'd be well fed if nothing else. Then a terrible thought came to me and I had to put down my bread and jam.

"Oh dear," I cried, going red with the shame of it. "If the curers won't take us on, we'll get no fixing money. I'll have nowt to pay you for my lodgings, Rachel."

"No," Mary Jane agreed, looking worried. "That's true enough."

Nelly went on eating steadily.

"Ey lass, haven't you enough to worry about?" Rachel shook her head. "Now drink up your tea and stop getting yourself into such a bother over nowt. It's up to me to see that you get fixed up, if I'm worried about my rent money. But do you not think I'd give food and a bed to Annie Lythe's lass without payment. Now eat up and shut up afore you get me cross."

I stared down at my plate then, feeling terrible. When I glanced back up at Mary Jane, my cheeks all hot and red, she grinned at me and winked. I picked up my bread and jam again.

"Thank you, Rachel," I said.

We ate on in silence, till all at once a great commotion came from Trickey's cottage.

"Here they come," Rachel told us. "Wait for it! They've been out parading round town in their best clothes today."

There was the tramp of feet on the stone cobbles outside, the sounds of loud voices and laughing; the floorboards started creaking and doors banged as the Scotch girls arrived back next door.

We had to smile at each other.

Mary Jane got up from the table and looked out of Rachel's kitchen window.

"Oh lor', Dory!" she squealed. "The boats . . . the boats are setting off."

I jumped up, and ran to join her. "Our Robbie!" I said. "I meant to look for him and I'm too late."

"No you're not," Rachel told me. "Leave these pots, and run down the path to the ladder. You can get onto the pier from here, and watch all the Whitby boats as they pass. Go on! You'll have to hurry! You can wave to the *Whitby Rose* for me."

I ran down the path to the edge of the cliff, and I almost had to close my eyes as I walked the wooden bridge that Rachel called the ladder. It sloped down from the cliff edge to the pier, carrying me over a great space, with rocks beneath and the sea swilling back and forth as the tide turned. Mary Jane came pounding along behind me.

"Ooh . . . I don't like crossing this," I called back to her.

"Just keep your Robbie in mind," she shouted.

I breathed out with relief as my feet touched the solid stone slabs of the pier and hurtled on to the very end of it.

Two boats had passed already and most of the visiting fleet were already heading off to the fishing grounds.

"Oh let me see him . . . please let me see him," I whispered.

"Them's Penzancemen," Mary Jane shouted.

"How can you tell?" I screwed up my eyes to see better.

"You can tell by the double masts, and the PZ register mark on the side. Look!" she cried, hopping up and down beside me and pointing. "The *Whitby Rose*, David Welford's plosher. He's Rachel's husband . . . wave to 'im! Here's two Fifies with their brown sails and the sloping gaff rigg at the top. This un's from Lowestoft . . . see the cloth caps that the fellers wear."

"How do you know all that?" I asked, looking at Mary Jane with new respect.

"Our Sam's told me. He brought me last summer for the regatta. There he is . . . there he is now," she went frantic, waving and jumping up and down.

"Where? Where?" I begged, my head turning this way and that as the local boats passed quickly through the narrow harbour mouth and out into the open sea. They'd a steady westerly wind behind them.

"There," she yelled. "The *Esther Welford.*"

"Oh yes," I waved along with her at the Welford brothers and Sam Ruswarp, but I was disappointed for I'd thought for a moment that she'd seen our Robbie.

Then, as the last few boats passed out between the arms of the two piers, I did see a young lad with a familiar look to him, in the stern of a sturdy Whitby plosher.

"Robbie!" I yelled at the top of my voice.

The lad turned towards us and it was our Robbie.

I ripped off my woollen shawl and waved it wildly over my head.

"Dory! Dory!" I heard him shout. He spoke to one of the men beside him and pointed to me and waved, but the boat was moving fast away. I waved and waved till it was out of sight.

"Did you see him?" I asked Mary Jane. "It was him, wasn't it?"

Mary Jane stared after the wake of the boats. "Oh aye, it was your Robbie, but did you see who he was with?" Her eyes were wide with surprise. "It was the *Louie Becket* he was on."

"The *Louie Becket?*" I shook my head, it meant nowt to me. "I saw a big feller with a great bushy beard?"

"Aye. He's the old lifeboat man. You know the one . . . him as was the only one saved when the Whitby boat went down."

"Him?" I said. "Our Robbie with the old lifeboat man?"

"Aye," she spoke quietly, impressed. "I think your Robbie's done all right for himself."

We ran back up to Henrietta Street, and told Rachel how we'd seen our Robbie. She laughed when she heard that.

"I might of known," she said. "Wait till I tell Trickey! The old feller cannot resist the herring season. He's supposed to be retired and they've certainly retired him from his lifeboat work. He swore last summer that the herring catches were so poor, he'd not be going again."

"Well, there's no mistaking him," Mary Jane said. "And there was their Robbie as large as life on his boat."

"In that case, Dory, you can stop your fretting over Robbie," Rachel told me. "He couldn't be safer, and he'll be looked after, too. The old feller never had bairns of his own, and he's always had a fondness for the young 'uns."

"Yer'll not be sending him back to Sandwick now," said Nelly.

"No," I said. "I'll not even try."

I couldn't settle down to sleep that night, what with the strangeness of the room and Nelly snoring. The swish and lap of the sea was loud by our window, though the sound of it was a comfort to me.

We got up early next morning and bandaged up our fingers, for, as Rachel said, we had to look as though we meant business. Then we went straight round to the fish quay, carrying our oilies and boots.

Rachel spoke to two of the curer's men, but one said firmly that he'd more than enough. The other looked us up and down and said that I was nowt but a bairn.

"She's a big strong lass," said Rachel.

"Aye, but I can see by her face she's a bairn. Look now," he said. "If I need another team I'll consider them, but I've all I need at the moment."

We hung around on the harbourside, watching the Scotch girls turning up for work in a noisy huddle as the boats began to arrive back, with a fair catch of gleaming herrings on board.

I looked out for Robbie, but I couldn't see him or the *Louie Becket*.

"Come on," said Rachel. "We'll go and get us a bite to eat, for there's nowt doing here."

We followed her back to Henrietta Street, feeling a bit down, and sat ourselves by the fire in Rachel's kitchen.

It was warm and spotlessly clean in there. Rachel had three freshly washed aprons drying by the fireside on a strange looking wooden clothes horse with three spindly legs. I frowned at it; the washing reminded me of Mam, and there was something familiar about that clothes horse.

We sipped the hot tea that Rachel handed out to us, and we were just beginning to unwind our bandaged fingers when there was a shout from the street and hammering on Rachel's door. Trickey came pounding up the hallway stairs.

"You want to get those lasses down to Pier Road," she shouted.

"What!" We all jumped up from our seats.

"There's a right old to-do," she panted, trying to get her breath, her eyes wide and excited.

"What's it all about?" Rachel asked.

"There's a Scotch lass sacked for bulking!"

"Now's your chance," Rachel cried, leaping up to grasp her shawl. "Get your oilies and boots and run as fast as you can."

We didn't need telling twice. We grabbed our things and pelted down through the streets to the bridge. But just as we got there, they closed the gates so that three tall masted herring boats could pass through into the upper harbour.

We cursed and swore and jostled each other and jumped up and down on the spot.

"Look over there," Rachel cried, pointing to Pier Road. "I can tell there's trouble from here. Listen to them Scotch lasses shrieking?"

"What is it that they've done wrong?" I asked fearfully.

"Bulking," Rachel told me. "It's the packer that's at fault. She's been chucking the herrings into the barrels all anyhow, then covering it up with a neat layer at the top. They can fill the barrels quicker that way, but it's not allowed. Oh no, you're sacked on the spot for bulking."

I caught my breath. It didn't seem such a terrible thing to me.

Then as soon as the bridge was back in place, we were off running over it and down to Pier Road.

When we got close I slowed up, my heart pounding with fright. I didn't fancy taking the place of a girl who'd been sacked. All the gutters had stopped their work and they were bellowing and shouting and shaking their fists at the foreman. Their speech was so different that it was hard to understand, but their meaning was clear enough.

"Gi'er another chance, Willie!"

"Couldna ye give 'er another chance?"

"She's had all the chances she's going to get." The man wouldn't be budged.

"Then we sh'll come wi'ye, Maggie!" Another girl shouted.

"Aye. We'll nae work for ye Willie if Maggie's sacked. We'll be off to Scarborough. They're crying oot for lassies there. We wouldna stay wi'oot ye, Maggie!"

And suddenly there were three big lassies, unfastening their aprons and marching away from the long wooden farlanes of herrings.

Rachel was in there quick as a flash, pushing us forward. "You said my lasses could have the next chance."

"Aye," the foreman sighed and scratched his head. "So I did. I'll try them, but they'll be on their own. It's all Scotch lasses down here on Pier Road you know. The Whitby teams are by the upper harbour."

"We're not bothered," Nelly said.

"Well, they'll not be fixed till I see how they work. Right, lass," he pointed to me. "Get behind that farlane and let me see thee gip."

Chapter 10

I struggled into my apron, my hands shaking horribly. I knew he'd picked on me because he thought I looked least able to do it. Quite a crowd had gathered about us.

"Look ye noo, he's teking on wee bairns," one of the Scotch girls muttered.

"Back to yer work," the man bellowed, and reluctantly the women turned again to their troughs.

I took the sharpest knife from my pocket and picked up a good-sized fish, trying hard to remember what Hannah had taught me. I pushed the knife in carefully and twisted it, and the guts flew out into the gut tub.

The man grunted. "Now size?" he snapped.

"Mattiefull," I answered him, my voice all shaky.

"What?" He put his hand to his ear.

"Mattiefull," I said it loudly.

He nodded and pointed to the basket behind me. I slipped the fish in and snatched up another herring to gut.

Nelly pushed in beside me and set to work. Mary Jane went to pack the barrel behind us.

"That one'll have to be packed again," the man said.

Mary Jane nodded, she began pulling the herrings out and setting them gently in a basket. The cooper went to help her.

I paused to watch Nelly for a moment and my mouth dropped open. Nelly could certainly gip, and she could gip fast. She'd done four fish while I did one.

"Stop gawping," she muttered under her breath. "Get gipping!"

"I'll try 'em for a week," the foreman told Rachel. "But that young un'll have to come into speed or she's out, and there'd better be no bulking."

"Then I'll be needing a week's food and rent money," said Rachel, holding out her hand to him.

The herring catch wasn't huge, but by the time we'd emptied our farlanes at the end of the day, I felt as though I'd gipped the whole of the ocean.

My back ached, my legs ached, my hands were sore and swollen and I'd gathered three cuts that stung with the salt that the coopers sprinkled onto the herrings. Mary Jane and I took turns at packing and it brought us a bit of relief, though we had to pack the fish in perfect neat layers. The foreman kept watching us and checking in case we grew careless. All the while the Scotch girls frowned at us and looked on with suspicion.

One of the young coopers was kind to us. He was a strong, broad-built lad, who lifted the barrels as though they were bairns and whispered good advice that we gratefully took. The coopers' job was to make the barrels and see that they were carefully packed, with just the right amount of salt sprinkled between the layers of herrings. Then they'd stack the filled barrels up neatly behind us for the herrings must be left to pickle for ten days.

I was so tired and hungry by midday that I thought I'd faint, and yet I knew that there was no stopping to eat or drink. I almost cried with relief at the sight of Rachel coming down Pier Road with a jug of warm broth and three bowls. It was the best broth I'd ever tasted, even though we had to take it in small quick sips while we stood at the farlanes.

Nelly gipped fast and steadily all through the day. She said little but she plodded on through the work like a donkey. I was glad to have her there with us, and I knew how right Miriam had been when she called her a tough 'un.

"Is that it?" said Mary Jane, stretching and rubbing her back.

"Aye," said Nelly, carefully wiping her knives and putting them into her pocket.

"I thought I'd die," said Mary Jane. "I'm sore all over."

"My legs won't stop wobbling," I groaned. "I swear I can't walk back to Henrietta Street."

"Yer'll manage," said Nelly. "That were a slow day. I've seen 'em gip three times that lot."

"We'll want you back at six in t'morning, to help wi' topping up," the foreman told us. "Don't you be late."

We rinsed our hands at the pump, and then set off walking slowly back to Rachel's house, a gang of the Scotch girls following behind us.

They shouted rude remarks at our backs and most of it I couldn't understand, but it was clear that they felt bitter about us taking the place of the girls that had gone, and I was scared of them.

At last, as we reached our door, one of the girls shouted out loudly so that we couldn't ignore it.

"You lot took Maggie's job fra her, we di'nna like that, ye ken. Wee bairns taking work fra those puir lasses that need the money."

I wanted to rush into Rachel's house and get away from them but Rachel herself opened the door. She'd clearly heard it all and she caught me by the arm.

"No," she said. "We've to sort this out."

She marched up to the women, dragging me reluctanctly along with her. Nelly and Mary Jane followed slowly.

"Now lasses," she said, "it's not as it seems. We didn't wish your Maggie sacked, but these lasses *do* need the money bad. We had to grab at the chance. Dory's mam is sick, and cannot earn. Her father was drowned a few years back. Now you lasses know well what that means to a family."

The girls looked down and shuffled their feet.

Rachel went on, while I hung my head. "For this lass, it's the gipping or the workhouse. Aye and all her little brothers and sisters, too."

I took a deep breath and lifted my head to face them. "I didn't like to take your Maggie's job," I said. "I didn't like it at all."

The Scotch girl sighed. "Di'nna fret, hinny. I do believe ye." She gently touched my cheek. "We'll forget it noo," she said.

"Aye, we'll forget it noo," the others agreed. They went quietly into Trickey's cottage.

"They'll be all right," Rachel said, as we turned back to her door. "They're grand lassies really and wonderful the way they work. We don't like to fall out wi' them for they bring us good rent money each summer, and they don't ask much for it. Now," she said, back to her usual practical self, "oilies and boots outside and straight to your room. I'll fetch your water and your supper to you."

Nelly flopped down on her bed in all her muck, and lay like that until Rachel appeared with washing water and cloths and a good supper of fish stew.

"You surprised me, Dory!" Mary Jane grinned. "That were brave of you to speak up to them like that. It's not like you."

"No," I shook my head. "I don't know what come over me. My fingers hurt so much I don't seem to care for owt else."

Nelly ate fast, then flopped back onto her bed again. Though I ached with each movement, I unwound the bandages and tried to wash my hands and put Mrs Love's ointment on my cuts.

"This water's going cold, Nelly, will you not wash?" I asked.

"No point," said Nelly and closed her eyes. "I'll wash meself on Sunday."

"Will you not change into your nightdress, Nelly?" Mary Jane asked, wrinkling her nose and pulling a face at me.

"Nobbut a waste o' time," Nelly muttered, already half asleep.

We were stiff as boards next morning when Rachel looked in to wake us.

"Come on," she called, grinning at the groans that came from us. "Aye, you'll be stiff I daresay, but there's only one way to be rid of it."

"What's that?" Mary Jane asked hopefully.

"Work on, hard and fast," Rachel told her.

That second day was even more difficult than the first, for the catch was good and we had to struggle through our stiffness and try to build up speed, but by the end of the day we all walked back to Henrietta Street feeling happier.

I was pleased for I'd seen our Robbie and he was mad with delight when he saw me gipping at the farlanes. He stood beside me for a hour or so chattering on and on about the fine time he was having fishing out of Whitby. I told him that I couldn't stop my work and he helped by pushing the herrings towards me.

"You should see them, Dory," he shouted. "You should see them silver darlings when we're scudding the nets. We haul them in, and they come flying at us, through the air and into the boat. They're everywhere! We're up to our knees in fish and covered in scales. And the smell, Dory! You wouldn't believe the smell!"

"Oh Robbie," I fussed. "Are you all right? Are you treated well?"

"Am I treated well?" he asked, a great smile on his face. "The old feller treats me like I'm his own lad. I make the tea for them," he said, beaming with importance. "And I make a good plum duff, boiled up in old condensed milk tins, for they need something warm and solid to fill their bellies out there."

"And can you do all that, Robbie?"

"Aye, I can. They've taught me how, and they never slap me if I spill. They just bellow at me and laugh."

"Oh Robbie," I worried. "It seems you've grown all of a sudden."

"Aye," he answered me sadly. "You've grown too, Dory. I would never have thought to see you working like this at the farlanes, and nagging at me just as if you were my mam."

Mary Jane was pleased that day, for suddenly there was a face we all knew well, staring open-mouthed at us on the harbourside: Liza Welford, done up in smart nursemaid's clothes of good grey cloth all neatly buttoned. She'd a young boy dressed in a sailor suit held firmly by the hand on one side of her, and a tiny girl in silks and ribbons on the other side.

Mary Jane grinned and shouted. "I told you I could gip a herring, Liza Welford."

"I cannot believe my eyes," Liza gasped and stared at us, but the young boy pulled at her.

"Ice-cream," he shouted. "Want some ice-cream."

"Just a moment, Master Rupert," Liza spoke patiently. "These are my friends."

The boy looked up at us puzzled. "Are they trades-people?" he demanded. "Phew! They smell! Mama says I mustn't speak to tradespeople. Stop talking to them and get me ice-cream. I'll tell Mama of you!"

Liza smiled rather sadly at us and shrugged her shoulders.

"I'll be back tomorrow," she called as the boy dragged her away.

We were glad to see her, and impressed by the elegance of her clothes, but we agreed that Liza did not seem at all happy. I'd never heard a young child speak to Liza like that. In our small school up at Bank Top, Liza Welford's word is law.

"What that one wants is a good hiding," Nelly said.

Nelly seemed to be in an unusually cheerful mood that day. She was quite chatty to us as we staggered our way back to Henrietta Street.

"Them Scotch lasses has been fine today," she said.

"Aye," I smiled. "That lass that shouted at us last night, she showed me how to drain off the pickle juice through the bunghole this morning, and she showed me how to pick the best fish for topping up the barrel. She was right kind to me and said to call her Jeanie."

"Aye," said Nelly, a secretive smile on her face. "And what about that big strong chap that works as our cooper. He says his name is George. He told me that as he filled our farlane and then he called me pet."

Mary Jane giggled. "He comes from Blythe. They call everyone pet up that way."

But the smile stayed there on Nelly's face.

"He called me pet," she said. "And he called me darling."

Chapter 11

We struggled on through the next few days, and by the time we'd cleared the farlanes on the Saturday night, we were dead on our feet.

"I'm gipped . . . as well as these herrings," Mary Jane grimaced at us, stretching to ease her back.

"I don't know what you're complaining about," said Nelly. "All these Scotch lasses are upset at the small catches."

Greater catches of herrings meant more money earned by us; for each team was paid by the number of barrels they managed to gut and pack. That week, I was grateful that the catches weren't huge for I couldn't have worked faster or harder than I did.

I grew to love the walk back to Rachel's cottage each night. Though my feet and my back ached and my fingers were swollen and stinging, still the relief at the end of the day was wonderful. Rachel's generous stews and puddings tasted as good as any fancy food we could dream up and the thought of them roused my spirits.

That first Saturday night, Jeanie's team, who'd been walking behind us, shouted wildly as we reached our door.

"What is it now?" I asked Mary Jane, nervously.

"I can't tell a word they're saying." She giggled as she wearily started to peel herself out of her smelly, crusted pinafore. "They get so excited and they talk so fast. If they'd only calm down and talk a bit slow."

It was Nelly that went to them. She listened frowning, then suddenly smiled back at us.

"Ceilidh?" she said. "Aye, I know what that means."

"What is it?" Mary Jane demanded.

"It's a bit of singing and dancing," Nelly told us, her eyes gleaming at the thought of it. "And the coopers are coming over to Tate Hill Pier."

We rushed then to get out of our oilies, and kicked off our boots by Rachel's doorstep.

After we'd had our supper we made good use of the washing water that Rachel brought to us, and got ourselves as clean and tidy as we could. Then we hurried down to Tate Hill Pier.

At first we sat and listened to a band playing on the far side of the harbour. The strains of music and the steady beat of the drum came to us clearly across the calm water.

We could see the coopers gathered by the bandstand and some of the Scotch girls. They'd lodgings on Burtree Crag, on the Westside, where they rented little rooms like ours from the fishermen's wives. Most of them were packed five or six into a room, and I knew that our lodgings with Rachel were spacious beside theirs. They kept waving at us, and when the bandsmen packed away their instruments and left, the coopers and the lasses came over the bridge to join us. Two of the lads had brought their squeeze boxes and another had a mouth organ. They settled themselves on the solid stone slabs of Tate Hill Pier and began playing tunes that were familiar to us all. It wasn't long before the fishermen came leaping ashore from their boats to join in with the singing.

There were Cornishmen, Scotchmen, and the Lowestoft men in their best Norfolk jackets and cloth caps. There were others like our cooper George who'd come down from Northumberland. They chattered and sang together in their different voices, making a fine and funny mixture of sounds.

Nelly was full of cheek and asked George outright if he were married.

He shook his head and smiled.

"Are yer courtin' then?" she demanded.

73

"Why no, pet," he said. "Are y' offering?"

Nelly suddenly went quiet and pink in the cheeks, while all the fellows laughed and hooted. I'd never seen Nelly look shamed before.

It was a beautiful summer evening; still and warm. I forgot my tiredness and wished that it would go on for ever. Even the old women came out from their cottages and sat by the harbourside knitting and nodding their heads to the tunes they played. As dusk fell, lamps were lit everywhere, for all the boats had crowded into the harbour for the weekend. The golden shimmer of their riding lights reflected in the water and the boats creaked gently as they rocked up and down to the wash of the waves.

Our Robbie came running down over Tate Hill sands with the old lifeboatman striding after him.

"I've found our Dory!" he yelled, and flung his arms round me. The old fellow went to gossip with Trickey and Rachel who'd brought their knitting outside.

The singing and clapping grew loud and jolly and some of the lasses got up and danced.

George held out his hand to Nelly. "Come Nelly, dance wi' me, pet. I never meant to give offence."

Nelly didn't need asking twice.

Soon me and Mary Jane were skipping along with them, though I don't know where the energy came from. One young Scotch girl sat alone and would not join in.

"What's up wi' her," I nudged Mary Jane and pointed.

"She's one o' them that's come down from Stornaway," said Mary Jane. "See her black scarf. Jeanie told me she only speaks the gaelic."

I stared at her. I could see from her face that she was young, no older than me. I was homesick enough, just coming down from Sandwick. I couldn't imagine what it must be like to travel so far from your home to such mucky work.

"Jeanie, Jeanie," I called as she whirled past with one of the coopers. "Will the Stornaway lass not dance?"

"Och, Katrina," Jeanie shook her head. "The poor bairn's nae left her home afore. We try oor best to look after her, but her faither has made her promise to keep herself away fra the laddies. She keeps to her word like a wee saint."

"Poor soul!" said Mary Jane. "Will she dance with us? We're not the laddies?"

"Ye canna do harm to try," Jeanie nodded.

So we went and stood in front of Katrina and we held out our hands to her. At first she would not budge, but as we kept on at her, with daft bits of miming and prancing around, at last she giggled and gave in. We took both of her hands and skipped round together until she was pink-cheeked and laughing.

"How can I skip like this when my feet hurt so?" I yelled at Mary Jane.

"I can't feel my feet at all," she grinned.

When at last we could stand no more, we flopped down by Robbie who sat with the lifeboatman.

"I wish Liza Welford were here to see all this," said Mary Jane. "Would they let her out on a Saturday night, do you think?"

I shook my head. I somehow didn't think that they would.

"I wonder if she can hear all this singing, up in her fine room," I said.

Just at that moment we seemed to have more in common with a Stornaway fisherlass who couldn't even speak to us, than any of those fine English folk who stayed up there on the West Cliff.

The dancing faded out, and Jeanie stood up to sing.

"Who'll buy my fresh herrin'
they're bonny fish and wholesome farin.
Who'll buy my fresh herrin'
new pulled from the sea.

When you were sleeping on your pillows,
did you think of our poor fellows?
Darkling with the wildest billows,
pulling herrin' from the sea.

Who'll buy my fresh herrin' . . ."

She'd a lovely deep voice and we all listened quietly, and clapped her when she stopped.

"We sing out there, you know," said Robbie, his eyes bright in the oil lamp's glow.

"What, you sing at sea?"

"Oh aye," he said, "but singing is quite different out there, Dory. It makes me want to cry."

"Nay, Robbie. Why should it make you cry?"

"It's the quiet of the sea all around us. First we have the fuss of shooting the nets, but then we have to settle down and wait. It goes very quiet, Dory . . . too quiet, and that's when they start. One of the Cornishmen will pick out the tune on his accordion, and we listen for a bit, then one of the chaps will start to sing, and we listen again, then slowly, slowly we join in. The sound o' deep voices comes from all the distant boats and it grows and grows until the whole fleet is singing."

"Oh Robbie," I cried. "It sounds beautiful."

"Aye, it's grand," he said, shaking his head. "But they only sing hymns out there. I don't think it would seem right to sing owt else."

"Oh, I wish I could hear it," I said.

The old lifeboatman who'd been listening to us, leaned forwards and touched my arm. "Don't you fret, little lass. You shall hear the Cornishmen singing their hymns, for I believe they've arranged to have a service on the boats tomorrow."

Sunday was a quiet day, and even Nelly kept to her word

and had a good wash, though we knew the smell of herrings still clung to us and would not be washed away, however many rinses of fresh water Rachel brought. We dressed ourselves in our Sunday clothes and gathered by the harbourside to listen to the lovely sounds of the Cornishmen singing their hymns, just as the old fellow had promised. They'd carried a harmonium out onto Tate Hill Pier, and Mary Jane edged closer and closer to it. I saw her fingers twitching to the solemn rhythm of the hymns, her face lit up with pleasure.

When they'd finished, we went to help Rachel with the dinner. I'd never had such a fine meal in all my life. Rachel and her husband had invited John Jack Trevorrow, the skipper of one of the Cornish luggers who'd been coming to Whitby for many years, and us three lasses sat at the table with them in our Sunday-best clothes.

Like all the fishermen's wives, Rachel had her ornaments and brasses polished and displayed for Sunday. Her kitchen looked a treat, with the black-leaded cooking range shining like jet, and the strange wooden drying rack folded away neatly in the fire corner.

As soon as we'd finished our dinner, Rachel sent us down to John Jack's boat, the *Silver Star*, to carry roast beef and a jug of gravy to the four men and the young cook who made up his crew.

Mary Jane pulled faces at me.

"We're never going to get Nelly away from these Cornish lads," she mouthed.

But she was wrong, for though the Cornish lads were full of fun and cheek, Nelly was not her usual loud-mouthed, forward self.

Later that afternoon, we set off with Jeanie's gang, marching arm-in-arm up the Abbey stairs to look down on the town from the top of the East Cliff. When we'd had our fill of the fine view from up there, we set off to parade ourselves round town; then last of all we climbed the steep hill up

onto the West Cliff. All the other gipping girls did the same, and we yelled and cheered at the tops of our voices when we saw another gang of herring gutters coming towards us.

We caught a glimpse of Liza up near the Saloon Gardens with her charges. We greeted her loudly, but she seemed flustered.

"I've been told I've not to speak to you, nor any trades people," she whispered, her cheeks red with the shame of it.

This was not the brave Liza Welford that we all knew. I hated to see her so timid and anxious.

The boy pulled at her arm and pinched his nose rudely. "Mama said no speaking to stinky fish girls," he cried. "Get me more lemonade or I'll tell Mama."

Liza ignored him for a moment. "I've to take them both to the picture man's studio tomorrow," she said. "They're to have their portraits made."

"It's a good job he's a patient man," said Mary Jane. "Even he might have a job to make that one look sweet."

"Best go now," said Liza.

"Did you see that?" Mary Jane spoke furiously as Liza went off towards the gardens.

"What?" I stared about us.

"He kicked her. That spoilt brat of a child kicked our Liza on purpose, and she did nothing."

"I told you," said Nelly. "He needs a good clout."

"I'd throw the lemonade right in his face!" cried Mary Jane.

We went to chapel with Rachel for the evening service, and found it filled with Cornishmen. Their voices swelled the singing and made it very fine. We didn't argue with Rachel when she insisted that we should get an early night, even though we knew that Monday should be a quiet day for the men would never go out fishing on a Sunday night.

Chapter 12

On Monday we slept till seven o'clock, then went to help the coopers sort out the barrels ready to go to the railway station. We had to open up the bung holes to drain off the salty oil and fish juices from the barrels that had stood there pining and pickling for more than a week. Then we had to top the barrels up with more herrings and pour back the pining juice till they were full and tightly packed, with a layer of perfect herrings on the top and straw to protect them.

"Ye canna get a finer handcream than the pining juice," Jeanie told us.

She made us dabble our hands in the smelly stuff and rub it well in. Though it made my cuts sting for a while, I found she was right for, as it seeped in, my skin grew soft and supple.

George pegged down the barrel lids carefully. He patted the top fondly, proud of a well-made barrel, filled and finished just right.

"They'll keep for a good twelve month now," he said. "It's off you go for a nice train ride, my fine fat silver darlings."

We giggled for he sounded as though he spoke to his bairns, or even his sweetheart.

"Hey Nelly! You'd better watch out," said Mary Jane, full of sauciness. "This lad's in love with the little fishes."

Monday was an easy day, with no herrings arriving. There was no need to bandage up our fingers and our work was done by noon. So we went back to Henrietta Street and helped Rachel to cover all her ornaments for the week's work; then we settled to do our knitting by the harbourside, gossiping and watching the men load up the boats with food, and freshly mended nets.

The weeks fell into a hard pattern of work, though Sunday and Monday brought us some relief. I managed to come into a bit of speed, and the foreman agreed to keep us on till the season in Whitby ended. Though I managed to gip the herrings faster, I could not come near to the Scotch girls.

"Well noo," boasted Jeanie. "When ye've worked at the gipping as long as me, ye'll tern oot fifty or sixty herrin' a minute."

"Aye, so you say, so you say," said Nelly gutting steadily.

But we all knew that Jeanie was not far wrong.

Frank Welford came to the farlanes looking for us. He was pleased to see that we'd got work, and he told me that all was well at home and that my mam was certainly no worse.

Sometimes we'd have an early morning visit from the picture man. He'd turn up with his new box cameras slung about his neck, and he'd be there beside the farlanes just as we were getting going, or late in the evening when we were packing up. He took snap-shot pictures of us, as he called them, while we chatted to him, though we dare not stop our work to help him with his pictures.

"You should come to take our pictures at noon when the sun's bright and we're piled high with herring," we told him.

He smiled and shook his head. "I've an appointment to make a picture of a bouncing baby at noon," he said sadly, and looked at his watch and left.

The first time that he saw us, he bowed in surprise and raised his hat.

"Herring ladies from Sandwich, I believe."

Mary Jane giggled and smiled broadly. "Do you remember, sir, how you took my picture once, sitting on Plosher Rock along with Liza Welford? The print you gave us has pride of place on Mam's mantelpiece."

"How could I ever forget?" he said. "That picture won me a medal. It was the beauty of the models that did it, of course."

That made Mary Jane giggle even more.

The first few weeks of August seemed to pass very fast. Sometimes I'd get a great tightness in my stomach that brought a terrible homesickness. It came when I thought about my mam and Alice and the bairns, but the work was so hard that there just wasn't time to sit and fret about it, and at least I saw that our Robbie was safe and well.

It was the last week in August when the change came. The catches were down and there were a lot of anxious folk about. We all stood to lose from poor catches; the dealers, the curers, the fishermen, the coopers and the gipping girls. Then we had four terrible days, one after another, when the catch was downright poor.

Everyone was thrown into despair. The dealers were talking of giving up and moving down to Grimsby. The fishermen's wives were most upset at that; if the fleet moved south so early, the herring girls and coopers would have to follow them and they'd lose the rent money that they got as landladies. I was fearful, for I knew I'd be shamed to go back to Sandwick Bay with such a small amount of money to show for my efforts.

"Aye. It's not like it used to be," Rachel told me. "It's all fading away. There were summers when I were a lass that the herrings were so plentiful we didn't need the bridge to get us across Whitby Harbour."

I must have looked puzzled for Rachel laughed. "We didn't need the bridge see, there were so many boats all crowded into the harbour that you could cross the water just by stepping from boat to boat."

"No!" said Mary Jane. "Can that be really true?"

"I swear it's no lie," Rachel told us. "Folk just walked from one boat to another, especially at weekends. And there were days when the barrels of herrings were piled so high in Whitby streets that they had to put on special trains to carry them away. There were hundreds of wagonloads leaving for market every week."

"Then why are the catches so poor now?" I asked.

"My husband swears that it's these big new steam trawlers, dredging up the herring young and making it hard for the small boats."

Suddenly we were spending our days by the harbourside, watching the comings and goings, and the gansey that I was knitting our Robbie grew fast from my needles.

Fishermen stood around the harbour rail fretting and discussing the weather and the wind and the swimming of the shoals. The weather was hot, too hot some said. Too calm and still and heavy.

The Whitby men and those from Lowestoft were talking about fishing on Sunday to see if they could make up their losses. The Cornishmen were shocked at that and the Scotchmen didn't like it at all.

At last it was decided that the Cornishmen should hold a special prayer meeting in the Old Primitive Methodist Chapel, and it was agreed that there'd be no more talk of Sunday fishing till after the service.

We were sitting on Tate Hill Pier that evening, doing our knitting and wondering whether we should attend the service or whether it were best left to the Cornishmen, when the picture man came wandering up the beach, carrying his heavy black camera box. He walked slowly and he seemed to be looking behind the rocks and peeping into the boat sheds.

"Have yer lost summat?" Nelly shouted to him.

He looked up at us and smiled, scratching his head.

"I know it's ridiculous," he said. "But I've lost my legs."

84

We all giggled for he looked to have a fine pair of legs to us.

He laughed with us. "Wooden legs, camera legs." He chuckled. "I swear that I left them somewhere near Tate Hill Pier, one day in spring. It was a dreadful day, poured with rain, and I stashed them somewhere meaning to come back for them."

All of a sudden it came to me in a flash that I knew exactly where the camera legs were hidden. Rachel's clotheshorse that aired her washing by the fire had always looked somehow familiar to me. Now I knew why; it was just like the folding wooden camera legs that I'd helped the picture man carry so long ago in Sandwick Bay.

My mouth dropped open and my hand flew up to cover it.

"What's wrong?" Mary Jane asked. "You look as if you've seen a ghost!"

"I know," I said all blushing and excited. "I know where your camera legs are, sir, but I don't know what Rachel will say."

I explained it to him and he looked amused.

"A drying rack, you say?"

We all got up then, smiling about it, and we led the picture man back to Henrietta Street. Rachel herself was there, just finishing the whitening of her doorstep.

"There y'are" she said, and she bobbed to the picture man. "I've a kettle just boiling," she told him. "Won't you come in and take a cup of tea, sir. I were just making some for the lasses."

"That's most kind of you," he said, and we all trooped into Rachel's kitchen, and sat ourselves down. There, in front of the fire, was the strange drying rack with a couple of Rachel's petticoats slung over it to air.

The picture man clearly recognised his camera legs, and he nodded at me and smiled while Rachel made the tea. Then we all sat there, chatting on about the lack of herrings,

while we sipped at our tea and waited for the picture man to mention the drying rack.

At last he got up to go and he'd still said nothing to Rachel about it. I was puzzled as to what to do when Mary Jane came to the rescue.

"Rachel," she said. "He don't like to tell you, but the gentleman has lost his camera legs, and there they are in front of the fire, airing your petticoats."

"What!" Rachel went quite red and flustered.

"Pray don't upset yourself, dear lady," the picture man said. "I don't need them after all, and you have found such a good use for them. I'd be pleased if you'd keep them."

"Oh heavens!" said Rachel, crossing the room and whisking her petticoats off the wooden camera legs. "Why ever did I not realise? I found them down by Dryden's boatshed. I thought the tide had washed them up. I was sure I'd find a use for them for they're made of good strong varnished wood."

"And you have found a use for them. As good a use as I. I'd be delighted if you'd keep them now."

Rachel hesitated just for a moment, then she firmly folded up the camera legs and handed them to the picture man, smiling comfortably now.

"You take them back," she said. "For I can air my petticoats on any old piece of wood, but you need these to fix up that camera of yours."

He took them then, and thanked her for the tea, and went off happily down Henrietta Street. We laughed when he'd gone.

"I thought he were never going to take them," said Mary Jane.

"Ey dear," said Nelly. 'He's a daft 'un. Fancy not wishing to tek his own belongings."

"Not daft," said Rachel. "Not daft at all. He's what I call a proper gentleman."

Chapter 13

We went along with Rachel and her husband to the service, but we could not even get inside, the chapel was so crowded. We stood out on the street and joined in the singing. The Cornishmen were in good voice and we sang for all we were worth.

My eyes filled up with tears as the service finished with the hymn my dad loved best of all. I remembered how he used to bellow out the words in his deep voice at the back of our small chapel in Sandwick Bay, so that folk turned round to look at him, and Mam would stick her elbow in his side to quiet him a bit.

The powerful words and music poured out of the small chapel and filled the streets and alleyways.

> Will your anchor hold in the straits of fear,
> When the breakers roar and the reef is near;
> While the surges rave, and the wild winds blow,
> Shall the angry waves then your bark o'erflow?
>
> We have an anchor that keeps the soul,
> Steadfast and sure while the billows roll;
> Fastened to the rock which cannot move,
> Grounded firm and deep in the saviour's love!

As we walked back to Henrietta Street, it turned cooler and a chilly wind started to blow.

"Well, let us hope all that singing and praising does some good," Rachel said, and I silently echoed her prayer.

David Welford sniffed at the wind. "This breeze comes off

the heather," he said. "A good north-westerly, I swear. Maybe these Cornishmen know what they're about."

"Well," said Mary Jane. "I've never known prayers answered fast as that."

The wind grew strong, and the town was filled with excitement. Some of the herring boats put out to sea at once, though others hesitated, fearing it might turn into a gale.

As the blast grew stronger and the sea rough, the herring drifters that were anchored out in the sea roads ran for the safety of the harbour. The tide was on the turn and it would not be long before the shallow water would make the harbour entry difficult. We wrapped our shawls around us tight, and stood up on the cliffside watching them.

"By the heck!" David Welford said. "When these Cornishmen sing up a storm, they don't muck about."

As dusk fell, two luggers and three of the coble boats that had bravely gone out to sea as soon as the wind rose were seen heading back through rough water.

We ran along to the cliff ladder to see them better.

Mary Jane clutched my arm. "Dear God!" she cried. "Look at that!"

The sea swilled through the space beneath the cliff ladder with a violent force even though the tide was going out. The luggers made the harbour safely, and the three cobles following came steadily towards the welcoming outstretched arms of the harbour. The small boats were tossed fiercely as the waves grew, it was hard going for them, we could all see that, and I clenched my fists up tight as we watched them.

"Can we not do summat!" I said.

Suddenly a rocket was fired on the far side of the harbour.

"See!" cried Rachel, pointing to the beach beyond the West Pier. "Thomas Langlands has set the lads to launch the life boat."

"Aye," her husband had to shout, for the wind snatched his voice away. "They've got a job on mind. I wonder whether to go to help. They'll be done by the time I get round there."

"You stay put," Rachel told him firmly. "They've plenty o'lads, and look – they're already off down the slipway."

We watched from the very point where the ladder joined the cliff as they hauled the lifeboat over the sand and out into the rough sea.

The men who pulled on the ropes were up to their waists in swirling water.

"Ah," David sighed, as the boat breasted the waves. "They're off! He's done well, has Thomas."

I was frightened standing out there, so near the cliff edge. The force of the wind drummed away behind us, pushing us closer to the edge at every blast, but I couldn't go back till we'd seen the cobles safely in.

The lifeboat stood by, and a cheer went up from the great crowd of watchers that had gathered as the first coble reached the safety of the harbour mouth. But almost at once a dreadful groan came from all around, for the two following cobles had been knocked sharply off-course as two cutting waves collided and rose high into the air. For a sickening moment both the boats were lost to our sight.

I cried out loud and grabbed tight hold of Mary Jane's shoulder. "Are they over?"

"Nay," she said. "But they're like to be."

Then we saw them again, both boats driven behind the great bulk of the East Pier close below us.

"The rocks!" David Welford cried. "They'll run aground. They cannot get the lifeboat round here, too shallow by far. We'll have to drag 'em off, Rachel."

And with that he was leaping down the precarious cliff ladder, over the water that crashed through the gap and down to the pier.

"Fetch all them lassies from Trickey's house!" Rachel shouted to us. Then she hurried after her husband.

"I'll get them," Nelly cried.

"Come wi' me," Mary Jane bellowed and snatched at my arm. "They'll be needing a great gang." Then she turned to run down the cliff ladder after Rachel.

I heard cries, shouts, and the sound of running feet behind me. People were pounding their way up Henrietta Street and heading for the ladder; they'd seen the need for help. I was terrified, but they'd be needing plenty of us if there were any hope of dragging the boats away from the rocks and keeping the coblemen out of the wretched sea.

I stepped onto the wooden ladder and made myself move forward, though it rocked with the fierce wind. Then I froze as I looked down at the drop beneath and the sea that roared and slavered below me like an angry starving beast.

I must move on, for folk were coming up fast behind me and I could be thrown over the side in the panic and rush, but the drop was so deep and the sea so wild that terror gripped me. It was Rachel that made me move. I think she'd seen that I was stuck, all iced-up with fear.

"Dory!" she cried. "Get down here now! It's the *Louie Becket*! We need you!"

That was it! That did it! Our Robbie was on that boat. I couldn't leave Robbie to be tossed into the sea, or crushed on those rocks. I stepped forward and, though the ladder seemed to swing wildly, I stared ahead through the gloom and the gale, making myself walk on till at last I stepped out onto the solid slabs of the pier.

David Welford had managed to snatch up a rope that they'd thrown from the *Louie Becket*. He handed it to Rachel, and then went teetering on the edge of the pier to catch a rope from the second boat.

"Help me!" Rachel shouted, lurching towards the pier side, dragged by the weight of the boat and the strength of the waves.

We ran! Mary Jane grabbed at the rope and I clung onto Rachel, gripping her round the waist. I caught a glimpse of our Robbie's white face below us. He was clinging to the side of the boat.

"Never fear," Rachel bellowed in my ear. "I can see 'em both. The old feller has him by the braces."

All I could do was cry out stupidly. "It's me as stitched those braces."

"Let's pray you stitched 'em well," said Mary Jane.

We struggled to hang on tight for what seemed like ages, but at last when Trickey arrived with Jeanie and the other Scotch girls, we knew that we'd enough help to keep the rope safe, and we started to haul the coble towards the curved tip of the pier.

As we rounded the tip we had to be careful and listen well to David, who told us when to pull and when to stop, for we'd so many folk on the pier all heaving and hauling that we were in danger of falling into the sea ourselves. The old lifeboatman and his men kept the *Louie Becket* clear of the stone pier with their oars. Robbie was grinning and yelling with excitement, while the plosher pitched and tossed in the darkening water. I don't think he knew what danger he was in.

When at last we had the *Louie Becket* safe inside the harbour, I ran straight up the cliff ladder without a thought, and down to the sands where people had gathered to help the men out. I ran to them, careless as to whether the second coble was saved or not.

Once we'd got them safely up to Henrietta Street, Rachel and Trickey flung open their warm kitchens to the drenched fishermen. Robbie and the old feller were soon sitting by our fireside, wrapped in warm dry blankets sipping broth.

I hugged my brother, while he grinned at me.

"Oh Robbie, I was so scared."

"Aye," said Mary Jane. "All she'd do was fret about your braces."

"Now Robbie," the old fellow chuckled, and wiped the broth from his beard. "I've always said braces is unlucky on a fisherman, but it seems yours have saved your life."

Though the storm carried on and the noise of the wind wouldn't let us sleep, Rachel sent us off to our beds, saying that Robbie and the old feller must stay till morning. We lay there whispering restlessly until a great crash and the sound of splintering wood sent us jumping out of our beds in the early hours. We ran to the small window near my bed and stared out through the dim light of dawn. The wind had dropped, but we could see the great mast of a ship, tilted to the side, down beyond the pier. Again a loud cracking sound was heard and the mast juddered. It was clear that another ship had run aground.

"Rachel, Rachel," we called. "We must go down again. There's men will need help."

"Nay," Rachel shouted to us, coming into our room fully dressed with a bucket in each hand. She laughed and shook her head. "They don't need saving. Thomas Langlands and his crew have got them off and they're safe ashore. It's the ship breaking up that's banging and cracking so, and she's a collier. Now you know what that means, don't you, lasses?"

We all three smiled broadly. "Free coal!"

"Right," said Rachel. "Are you fit to help us then, for they'll all be down ... fast as you can say knife?"

We flung on our clothes and Rachel handed out buckets and baskets and sacks, but though we'd not wasted any time, we found that half of Whitby was down there by the rocks, slipping and sliding and grubbing about, up to their waists in blackened water.

All through the morning we clambered over the rocks picking up lumps of wet coal. By noon there was not a scrap of it left, though there were damp black trails all through the streets and alleyways, and folk with smeared faces, and hands and arms and aprons. Bairns carried baskets of coal through the streets to their grannies and everywhere there were smiling faces.

"They say God works in a mysterious way," said Rachel, with a laugh. "We ask for fish and he gives us coal. Now we've hope of keeping warm next winter."

The shiny black stuff was as good as lumps of gold, and whether the Cornishmen had sung up a storm of fishes or not, everyone was glad.

When the fleet set off that evening, there was a good crowd down on the piers to watch them go, with a steady westerly wind behind them. I stood there waving to our Robbie as he passed in the *Louie Becket*.

"Oh, I wish he wasn't going," I said. "Not after last night."

Mary Jane shrugged her shoulders. "It's their last chance,"

she said. "The dealers will surely go, if there's no better catch in the morning."

We slept well that night, for the wind had dropped and we were exhausted with all the upset and excitement that we'd had. Next morning we were up early and waiting hopefully at the farlanes before ever there was any sign of the boats coming in.

The dealers were restlessly walking up and down Pier Road, and the coopers and gippers all there and ready to work. At last there were shouts from the pier, and the sound of cheering. Most of the folk went running off down towards the harbour mouth.

"We should stay by the farlanes and wait," said Nelly.

"I'm not," said Mary Jane.

"I can't wait," I said, and hurtled off after her down towards the pier, pushing my way through the crowd.

There was a fine sight, all the drifters heading steadily back to harbour, mobbed by gangs of hungry herring gulls that wheeled and whimpered above them. One of the Whitby ploshers led them all.

"Look," Mary Jane yelled. "Look it's the *Louie Becket*."

I screamed out loud, bursting with pride, for there was our Robbie standing in the bows, up to his knees in a huge pile of gleaming herrings.

"Robbie! Robbie," we yelled, jumping up and down.

"Look, Dory!" he shouted. "Silver darlings! Hundreds of 'em, thousands of 'em."

Chapter 14

We had to run back fast to our farlanes then, for we'd be sacked if we were not there when the coopers came to fill them up.

It was a wild day that followed, what with dealers competing for the fish and the prices going up and up and us gipping for ever. The farlanes were piled high like I'd never seen them, and the smart visitors came down the steep pathways to gawp at us. They milled around, asking daft questions and getting in our way.

Though we were already tired by noon, there was such a spirit of rejoicing that I could not feel miserable. It was a warm sunny day and as we worked the fish seemed to fly through our hands. Glints of deep purple and blue glanced up into our eyes from the pattern of black diamonds on the herrings' backs, while the bright midday sun caught their creamy white underbellies, making them gleam with rainbow lights like mother of pearl.

"Treasure . . ." I murmured.

"Treasure all right," Nelly agreed with me for once. "Good as silver coins these are."

I went into a waking dream, my hands working of their own accord, not noticing any more the strong oily smell of fish and the dark red blood of the guts that spattered my face and arms.

When dusk fell we'd still got our farlanes piled high, and the fleet had set out to try their luck once more. George and the other coopers set up oil lamps between the farlanes so that we could see as it grew dark.

It started to rain and though we got soaked to our skins, still we gipped the herrings.

"How long must we go on?" I begged Jeanie.

"We've tae work till we've done, lassie," she told me.

It was then that exhaustion really hit me, I felt as though someone had been beating me over the shoulders, leaving me bruised and sore. I looked down and saw properly just what I stood amongst. My father's best sea boots were deep in fish guts so that I could not see them clear, my apron the same, and my arms crusted up to the elbows. Nelly stood beside me, crusted and filthy, steadily gipping away.

"Oh Jeanie," I said. "I cannot do it. I cannot gip another fish."

"Ye canna stop noo, lassie," she told me cheerfully. "Keep going, and we'll have a bit of a sing, tae cheer us. Turn the lamps up, George!"

The warm golden glow lifted my spirits, though the sooty smuts from the smoking lamps blew into our faces. Jeanie got us singing fast and loud.

> "Halibut for the swanky squire,
> Haddock for his wife,
> Cod is for the parson,
> Mackerel for long life.
>
> Ling is for the fisherman,
> Fishead stew for free,
> But the bonny salted herring,
> Is the only fish for me!"

We all joined in, smiling and laughing. The rhythm and the tune seemed to help us and, as our voices grew loud and rough, we gipped faster than ever.

> "Oh, we are jolly herring girls,
> A-salting all day through.
> We salt the silver darlings,
> And we'll do the same to you.

Oh, we are jolly herring girls,
A-gipping all day through,
We gip the silver darlings,
And we'll do the same to you.

Oh, we are jolly herring girls,
A-pickling all day through.
We pickle the silver darlings,
And we'll do the same to you."

The singing finished with wild cheers and screaming. At last, with thick darkness gathering around the glow of our oil lamps, we could see that we were coming to the end and emptying our farlanes.

I can't remember the walk back to Henrietta Street, though I seem to think that Rachel was with us. I think she must have carried us back. What I do know is that we all slept in our filthy clothes that night, glad of the bare rooms and brown paper covered curtains. None of us washed till the morning, and we didn't bother over-much then.

Next day the catches were up again, though not quite as much of a miracle as the day before. Though we ached and grumbled, everyone told us that the only way to get right was to work on, and so we did. It was at noon that day that we had a terrible bit of excitement.

The usual gang of visitors was gathering about to watch us at work, and even the picture man had deserted his studio to struggle through the crowd to make his snap-shots. Then we saw Liza Welford, there with her two charges.

"Liza! Liza!" Mary Jane shouted happily, though she never stopped her packing. "I thought the smelly fisherlasses were forbidden."

"Aye. So they are, but I don't care, I'm not missing this."

That sounded much more like the Liza that we all knew. She stood at the back of the crowd, holding the little lass up to watch our work. The boy climbed up beside her, close to the harbour rail pulling at her and whining as usual, though I could see that Liza told him to get down.

I was glad that I paused just for a moment in my work to smile across at them, for it was then it happened and I saw it clearly. One minute the lad was there, scratching and hot in his expensive sailor suit, the next he wasn't, and all I could see was the space by the harbour rail where he'd been.

I dropped the herring that I was gutting and I screamed at the top of my voice.

"Liza! The lad! He's fallen in the water!"

George had been sprinkling our fish with salt. He looked up at me as I screamed and just for one moment he stared into my face with horror, then he turned about and I've never seen anyone move so fast. He cut straight through the pushing crowd, leaping up onto the harbour rail, and vanished from sight after the boy.

"George!" A great frightened bellow went up beside me from Nelly. Then everyone rushed to the harbour rail.

The tide was in and the water was cold and deep, but George had the lad by the collar of his suit. The child came up, choking and spouting dirty harbour water, but George swam quickly to the nearest steps and they were both hauled out of the water by many willing hands. It was all over in a minute, and the big man was standing dripping on the quayside with the spluttering shivering lad in his arms.

"Liza! Where's Liza?" Mary Jane turned about, looking for her friend.

Though everyone else had stopped their work and rushed to the harbour side, Liza had not moved. She stood just where she'd been before, her face gone white as a ghost. She clutched the little lass so tightly that the bairn could scarce breathe, and she shivered as violently as though it were her, Liza Welford, as had been soaked in the water.

Mary Jane ran to her and threw her arms about her, fish guts and all.

"It's all right, love," she told her. "It's all right. The lad's as right as rain, just wet and fearful."

George followed her, carrying the lad who coughed and spluttered, his lips gone rather blue.

"Show me where you're staying," he said. "I'll carry the lad to his home, for I'll have to stop my work to go and change."

Liza just stared up at him, her eyes wide and wild.

"Let's get him back quickly, pet," George touched her arm. "Then he'll not take chill."

Liza seemed to come to then. She nodded, and turned to show the way.

"Come now, lass, let's run."

Mary Jane and I watched them go, reluctantly turning back to our farlanes. It was only then that we saw that Nelly was bent double over the fish troughs, and Jeanie beside her, fishing fresh bandages from her pocket.

"What is it, Nelly?" we cried.

"The puir bairn's got a nasty cut," Jeanie told us. "Och, what a day we're having!"

Nelly straightened herself, but all the colour had drained from her face. Blood poured down from the base of her thumb.

"'M all right," she muttered.

Jeanie shook her head. "I dinna call it right. Ye should go hame and get Rachel to clean it properly for ye."

"What's happening here?" the foreman came to ask. "Are you gipping herrings or what?"

He was answered by angry shouts and cries from all the Scotch girls.

"Can ye not see!"

"The lass has cut herself!"

"We'll work when she's taken care of and not before!"

The foreman sighed and Nelly picked up her knife.

"'M all right," she repeated, and snatched up a herring in the tightly bandaged hand and set about gutting it.

"I dinna like it," Jeanie muttered, but she went back to her work and we all followed her.

We worked on for the rest of the day and Nelly seemed to recover well, her cheeks soon pink again. It was a long day and we gutted on through the dusk, cheered by the number of barrels we filled and the thought of the money that they'd bring.

Rachel clicked her tongue when she unwrapped Nelly's bandaged hand that night. The cut was deep and nasty, and Nelly flinched as Rachel cleaned it up and smoothed on Mrs Love's ointment.

I don't think any of us were surprised when we heard a hesitant knock on Rachel's door, quite late that night. We didn't leave our beds, we were too tired, but we heard Liza's stumbling miserable voice.

"I'm so sorry, Aunt Rachel."

"Away inside, lass," Rachel told her calmly. "I know well enough what's happened. I've the bed place made up and ready for you."

It was good to find Liza looking comfortable in her old clothes, knitting furiously by Rachel's fireside when we got back to Henrietta Street after our work the next day. Rachel broke her rule and let us go up to the kitchen in all our muck just to see her for a while, though we'd to promise not to touch anything and not to sit down. Mary Jane was delighted to be back with her friend, though Liza was miserable. She kept going over it all and making herself feel worse and worse.

"How can I go back to Sandwick and tell my mam I'm sacked?" she said. "How could I have let it happen?"

"I don't think it were really your fault," I told her. "I saw the lad. He wouldn't get down. He wouldn't do as he were told."

"I shouldn't have taken him near the harbour," Liza shook her head. "Mam will be so shamed of me, and what will Miss Hindmarch think?"

"That lad had trouble coming to him," said Nelly. "He's maybe learnt summat."

But Liza would only shake her head and sigh. "I've lost more than half the wages I should've earned," she said. "Rachel says that I may stay for a day or two, but then I'll have to go home and face Mam. Do you know what they told me? That I was sacked for bringing him back, wet and smelling of fish! They didn't seem bothered about the danger, just the smell of fish!"

We could not help but smile at that, but Liza was tearful.

"How can Miss Hindmarch take me back as pupil teacher after this?"

"Why don't you write to her?" I said. "You're good at writing, Liza."

"That's a grand idea," said Mary Jane. "Write one of your beautiful letters to Miss Hindmarch and tell her all about it. It can't make things worse."

"Aye," said Liza, thoughtfully. "I'll maybe try."

The catches stayed good for the rest of the week and we worked like beasts. I think it was just the happy thought of the money that kept us going. Nelly gipped as steadily as ever, with her cut hand all bandaged up. It seemed to bother George.

"What made your knife slip, Nelly?" he asked. "You're as grand a gipper as any I've known. Was it the shock of the little lad falling?"

"Aye," said Nelly, blushing. "That were it."

Mary Jane grinned saucily at me. We both knew well what it was that had made Nelly go and cut herself, and it wasn't that spoilt little lad.

Chapter 15

Towards the end of the week, we began to worry about Nelly. When Rachel tended the cut hand each night, she shook her head at the puffy swollen flesh that was revealed.

"The curer's salt won't let it heal," she said. "It eats into the wounds, does that salt. I don't like the look of it, Nelly. You'd do best to let the doctor see it."

"I'm not working like this to spend my money on doctor's bills," said Nelly.

"Why not rest for a day and let Liza go in your place."

"She can't gip," Nelly was stubborn. "None of them can gip like me."

Though she didn't look at all well, we couldn't disagree with that. None of us *could* gip like Nelly.

We'd another good catch on the Saturday, and I was standing up at the farlanes in the hot midday sun. Nelly worked beside me, but she'd gone very quiet.

"Are you all right, Nelly?" I asked.

Beads of sweat covered her face, and her cheeks had turned red. The look of her frightened me.

"Nelly?" I said. "Are you sick?"

There was no answer, though she carried on gipping.

Then, all at once, the colour drained from her face and she keeled over, head first into the trough of herrings.

"George!" I shrieked, and he was there at once.

"Eh dear, eh dear . . . come on lass!" he muttered, pulling Nelly out of the trough. She was still senseless as he heaved her up into his arms. Both of them were covered with fish scales.

He carried her over to the harbour rail. "Give her some air!" he shouted, as people fussed around, curiously. I followed, trembling with the shock of it.

Jeanie dropped her gipping knife and rushed over to us. At last Nelly seemed to revive a little, but then her whole body took to shivering violently. She couldn't seem to stand or even speak, her teeth were chattering so.

"She shouldna be here," Jeanie said, worriedly pressing the back of her hand to Nelly's flushed cheek. "Take her straight back to her lodgings and see she's put to bed."

"Aye," George agreed. "Come on now, pet."

He put his arm round her waist, and set off towards the bridge, half-carrying the girl.

"Can he manage?" I asked Jeanie. "She's a big lass."

"Well, he's a big lad," said Mary Jane. She'd left the packing and come to see what was up. "I shouldn't laugh." She giggled.

"Noo, ye shouldna," Jeanie said, turning cross. "Ye'll noo be laughing if it's the blood poisoning, and I fear it is."

"Oh no," I cried. I didn't like the sound of that and my eyes filled up with tears.

"I dinna ken how ye'll manage withoot her," Jeanie rubbed it in.

We didn't know either, but we set to work again before the foreman noticed that we were short handed, both of us gipping together and taking turns to do a bit of packing now and then. Jeanie'd been right; we couldn't make half the speed that we'd had with Nelly and I despaired at the sight of the mountain of silver fish in front of me.

"Where's George?" Mary Jane complained angrily. "It's never taking him all this time to find Henrietta Street."

Suddenly tears poured from my eyes, I couldn't stop them, and my hands would not stop shaking as I tried to gip.

"We can't do it!" I sobbed. "We can't manage without Nelly!"

"Look at ye both," Jeanie sighed, leaving her own farlane

and coming to us. "Bairns, both o' ye. Didna I say it. Dinna fret, shove up and make space for me. We canna have ye pickling these fish wi' salt tears."

She set herself to gip our herrings at the speed of lightning.

"Oh thank you, Jeanie," I said, knuckling the tears from my eyes and trying to get on.

She shook her head. "I canna do it for long, lassie."

It seemed ages before George came back, but when he did he brought Liza with him, already wrapped in Nelly's oilskin apron.

"Nelly's awful poorly," she said. "She's in a right state and Rachel's putting her to bed."

"Oh, Liza," I begged. "Will you help us?"

"Course I will," she said. "But I'm not much good at gipping."

"You soon will be," said Mary Jane.

"Bless ye lassie," said Jeanie. "Set her to do the packing, George. Now you two must gip like the wind."

That night we found that Rachel had settled Nelly in the bed place in her kitchen, where she shivered and shook. Liza's belongings were dumped in our room.

We washed ourselves, then we went up to Rachel's kitchen to see if we could help. It was shocking to find our big strong Nelly weak as a bairn. She'd a rash on her cheeks and she was tearful, not at all herself.

"I'm sorry, lasses," she kept saying. "I'm so sorry."

I'd never heard Nelly apologise to anyone. It made me feel quite sad to hear it. She seemed to go from burning hot one minute to shivering cold the next.

"It's not contagious?" Mary Jane asked, looking alarmed.

Rachel shook her head. "It's as I've feared all along. The poison in that cut has got into her blood, and it's brought on a fever. She must rest and keep warm and quiet, and let me clean that cut each day. It's no good trying to gip with a wound like that."

"So we'll have to finish the season without her?"

"Aye." Rachel was firm about that.

"Well," said Liza cheerfully. "I came as a nursemaid, but it seems I'll go back as a herring girl."

"Do you mind?" I asked her.

"Nay, Dory," she put her arm about me. "It's better far than going home in disgrace."

On Sunday George came round to Henrietta Street and found us in a right taking. Sunday dinner and Sunday service were forgotten while we boiled up broth and herbs and brought bowls of fresh cooling water from the pump. None of it seemed to do any good; Nelly thrashed about in a high fever, shouting out at Rachel and calling for her mam. She stared wildly about her, knowing none of us, two hectic red patches on her cheeks.

Rachel was shaken from her usual calm. "I'm thinking Nelly should have the doctor," she told George. "Though she swore she would not. She keeps crying out for her mam, and I'm wondering if we should send for old Mrs Wright."

"Nelly shall have the doctor whether she likes it or not," said George angrily. "I shall fetch him, and I shall pay him too."

"Will he come visiting on a Sunday?" I wondered, doubtfully.

"I shall make sure that he comes," cried George.

He was back within the hour with the smart doctor who lived up on the West Cliff. The doctor was clearly annoyed to be dragged away from his Sunday dinner, but when he saw the state of Nelly, he spoke kindly and said we'd done right to call him. He sent George running round to the ice-cream man for ice to cool the fever. The doctor said it all depended on us keeping her calm and getting her to rest. He left a special mixture that he said would help.

George was the only one that Nelly would take notice of. While he sat beside her, holding her hand and murmuring gentle words, she'd be still and quiet; but as soon as he moved she'd grow wild again. Poor George sat there all night. In the morning we were relieved to find that she was sleeping peacefully and Rachel was hopeful that the worst was over.

Through the next weeks we worked on at the gipping with Liza in our team. First she did most of the packing, but gradually she began to work at the gipping, and I was very proud to find myself teaching her how to gut a herring. She picked it up quickly and, by the start of October, Liza was as fast as me and Mary Jane.

"Oh, Liza," I said. "We're missing school now, aren't we. It don't matter for me and Mary Jane, but what will Miss Hindmarch do without her pupil teacher? Did you write that letter?"

Liza shrugged her shoulders. "Aye. I wrote it, but I've heard nowt. I'm sure Miss Hindmarch will have had such bad reports of me that I can never face her again." Liza sighed and smiled. "At least my dad has told me that he's proud to see me gipping with the other girls and he says that he's explained it all to Mam."

Each evening George walked back to Henrietta Street with us to see Nelly. He examined the cut hand each day, saying that he'd seen many a nasty cut in his work, but few as bad as that one. Once she was up and gaining strength, Nelly would walk slowly down to Tate Hill Pier with him, and they'd sit there together, watching the busy harbour.

As the days passed, the work became more patchy and the catches dwindled. There'd be a bad day, and the drifter men would talk of moving down to Grimsby; then they'd have three days of decent fishing and they'd be cheered. All the talk was of the herring movement.

"They're taking off," David Welford told us.

"Aye, for sure," Rachel agreed. "The time has come, they're taking off; they're swimming south."

The Lowestoft men set off for East Anglian waters to chase the black noses, as they called the autumn fish that they caught down there. The Cornishmen stocked up their boats in readiness to follow them.

In the third week of October the dealers went, and the foreman told us that we'd be paid off at the end of the week. The Scotch girls were packing their kist boxes ready to take the train down to Grimsby, though some of them were going as far as Yarmouth and Lowestoft. We'd to top up the last lot of barrels on Saturday, then we were done.

When we got back to Henrietta Street on the Saturday afternoon, Rachel called us up into the kitchen, and said we'd got a visitor. There, sitting by the fireside, sipping tea from Rachel's best china, was our own Miss Hindmarch.

We were so surprised that all we could do was stare at her. She laughed and got up and kissed us all; she didn't seem to mind the smell of fish.

"I'm sorry, so sorry," Liza stammered. "I know I've let you down."

"Oh no," Miss Hindmarch told her. "I think it's quite the other way. I got your letter and I got another letter, too. My friend the photographer wrote to me. He told me how patient you'd been with that awkward little boy, and how dreadfully the child behaved when you visited his studio. How he'd grabbed at all the photographic plates and poked his fingers into the chemical jars. No I think it's *me* that let *you* down, Liza. The family were not at all what I'd thought, and the little boy was quite clearly pampered and spoilt. Now will you forgive me, and come back to Banktop School? I am missing my pupil teacher very much. Indeed, I cannot manage without you."

"Of course I will," Liza smiled happily.

Robbie came running down to Henrietta Street, all excited that he'd got his pay.

"I can't wait to get home and give it to Mam," he told me. "The old fellow says he's taking me back to Sandwick in the *Louie Becket*. He'll take you too, Dory, if you wish. He wants to visit Mam, he insists on it."

"That's right kind of him," I said.

Me and Mary Jane and Liza went to the railway station with Jeanie's gang to see them onto the Yarmouth train.

"Well noo, we're going to miss ye Yorkshire lassies, that's for sure," said Jeanie, hugging us one by one. "Will ye nae come doon for the herringing next year?"

"Aye. We'll come again," we told her.

When we got back to Henrietta Street, we found George and Nelly sitting together on Rachel's step, Nelly's arm comfortably linked through his. Nelly was looking well again, due to Rachel's careful nursing.

"George is off tomorrow," Nelly told us, smiling hugely.

"No need to look so pleased about it," Liza said.

"But then he's coming back," Nelly blushed.

"Oh! Do you mean . . .?" Mary Jane for once didn't know how to ask.

"Aye," said George. "I'm fixed to work till Christmas, but then I'll be coming back up north. I'll be calling in at Sandwick Bay and I'm hoping that me and Nelly will be wed."

I threw myself at Nelly then, hugging her for all I was worth. She looked surprised and pleased. I truly wanted her to be happy.

"You'll make a right couple, you two will." Mary Jane smiled at them. "Are we to be bridesmaids, then?"

"Can be, if yer like." Nelly looked coy.

It wasn't easy to share out the money that we'd earned. Mary Jane and I agreed that Nelly had a right to claim more than us, as she's carried us for the first few weeks. But Nelly was full of joy and kindness.

"Fair shares, fair shares," she insisted. "Liza and me shall split the third between us."

The payment that I got seemed a fortune to me, and Mary Jane had enough for a decent organ.

So the herring season came quietly to a close, and the Whitby men turned to bait their long lines once more, and braced themselves for the winter gales.

Epilogue

On a chilly afternoon in late October, we set out of Whitby harbour in two ploshers, dressed in our best clothes, heading for Sandwick Bay. I was so proud of Robbie, a proper fisherman he looked, wearing the new gansey that I'd just finished knitting in our special Sandwick pattern that we call the waves and herringbone. I went with him in the *Louie Becket*, and Liza, Nelly and Mary Jane followed in the *Elspeth Welford*.

I'd been worried about the journey, for when we'd come to Whitby in July, the choppy water had made me feel thoroughly sick.I'd almost wondered whether to insist on riding home in the carrier's cart, but then I reminded myself that as Father was a fisherman and I was now a herring girl, I should be shamed. I needn't have worried; the sea was calm, the water like silk, and as we turned towards our bay the sun came out from behind grey clouds and lit up a silver shining pathway before us on the water.

It seemed that half the village was expecting our arrival, for there were all the Welfords down on the staithe to greet us, and Miriam and Alice and Nelly's old mother, Mrs Wright.

"Mam, Mam," Nelly shouted at the top of her voice. "Mam, I'm getting wed."

"Now, young Dory. Don't you go splashing in the water, and getting your good frock all wet," the old lifeboatman told me kindly. He jumped into the water himself and lifted me out.

I ran to Miriam and Alice.

"Lord! I swear you're taller than ever, Lanky Dory,"

Alice squealed and I hugged her tightly, happy to be called Lanky Dory once again.

"How's our mam?" I begged Miriam.

"Well, you can go and see for yourself." Miriam laughed.

"She's there!" Robbie yelled beside me, pointing to the stone blocks that we used as seats outside the lifeboat house.

"Aye," said Miriam. "She's insisted on walking down the bank to greet you."

"What? She can walk?"

"She can. But it's slow and hard work for her. Go and see."

We both ran over the staithe to Mam, slowing a little as we got close, both of us gone suddenly shy.

"Wel . . . come home," she said. The words came slow and halting.

"Mam," I cried. "You can speak!"

She laughed and nodded. "Yes. Speak a bit."

She pushed herself up to her feet, and we both clung tightly to her, laughing and crying all at once.

Then we remembered the really important thing, and we brought out the money that we'd earned.

Mam began to cry, though I think it was happy tears.

"So proud of you . . . both," she said slowly. "Enough to . . . see us right through to the spring."

"Now Mam," I said firmly. "I don't want you to fret about money any more. Me and Robbie shall go to work with the herring fleet again next year, and I'm willing to wash and scrub right through the winter, so we'd better start taking in washing again."

Mam shook her head, smiling through her tears.

"Whatever's got into our Dory?" Alice cried out, amazed at my bossiness. "I thought you hated all that soap and water."

"So I did," I grinned at them. "But it's all changed. I'm different now. I'm a herring girl . . . I can do anything!"

Acknowledgements

The author and publishers would like to thank the The Sutcliffe Gallery, 1 Flowergate, Whitby, North Yorkshire for their helpful advice and permission to use Frank Meadow Sutcliffe's photographs on pages 5, 12, 27, 40, 52, 59, 78–9, 86–7, 91, 96–7, 113. They would also like to thank the Bradford Museum for permission to use the photographs for the frontispiece and on pages 3, 66, and 104.

'Bread on the waters' by Joe Tomlinson, North Sea fisherman, is a quotation from Dora Walker's book, *Freemen of the Sea*, published by A. Brown & Sons Ltd., 1951.

The author would also particularly like to thank:

The staff of Whitby Library
The staff of Whitby Archives Trust, Grape Lane, Whitby
Whitby Literary and Philosophical Society
Mr John Tindale
Mrs Anne Leadley
Mr Bill Fortune

Bibliography

BUTCHER, DAVID Following the Fishing, 1987 (Tops'l Books)

COOK, JUDITH Close to the Earth, (Routledge & Kegan Paul)

HILEY, MICHAEL Frank Sutcliffe: Photographer of Whitby, (Gordon Fraser)

HODGSON, W. C. The Herring and its Fishery, 1957 (Routledge & Kegan Paul)

MARSHALL, MICHAEL W. Fishing: The Coastal Tradition. (Batsford Books)

MINTER AND SHILL, I and R, Storm Warrior, 1991 (Heartlands Press)

TINDALE, JOHN Fishing out of Whitby, 1987 (Dalesman)

The Whitby Gazette 1901, 1902, 1903.

From THE SUTCLIFFE GALLERY:

Frank Meadow Sutcliffe, Photographer: A selection of his work compiled by Bill Eglon Shaw.

Frank Meadow Sutcliffe: A second selection compiled by Bill Eglon Shaw.

Frank Meadow Sutcliffe: A third selection compiled by Michael Shaw.